The Emperor
and the Butterfly

The Emperor and the Butterfly

Helen Aileen Davies

Matador
9 De Montfort Mews
Leicester LE1 7FW, UK
Tel: (+44) 116 255 9311 / 9312
Email: books@troubador.co.uk
Web: www.troubador.co.uk/matador

ISBN: 978-1905886-53-1

Typeset in 11pt Stempel Garamond by Troubador Publishing Ltd, Leicester, UK
Printed in the UK by The Cromwell Press Ltd, Trowbridge, Wilts, UK

Matador is an imprint of Troubador Publishing Ltd

To my parents, Rob, Angharad, Paul, Stephen, David, Vassilia, Tariq and Carolyn. Without you this book would never have been written. I love you all very much.

Thanks also to James Powell for the cover images and to Marian Keyes for her support and encouragement.

The Bag Incident

☙ ❧

It all looked so easy in films. Boy meets girl. Boy fancies girl. Girl fancies boy. Boy asks girl out. Girl says yes. They live happily ever after. Real life seemed to be a great deal more complicated. Rhys Harris rubbed his eyes and stared blearily at his computer screen. How was he supposed to concentrate on "The Effects of the Civil War on Welsh Society" when his head was full of Elen Lloyd? He studied the paragraph he had just written. He muttered under his breath. He had only written that "Elen" Pritchard had sided with the king instead of "Edward". He corrected his mistake. He stretched and turned to gaze at the copper coloured mountain which loomed protectively behind him. Autumn was setting in. The heather had turned to rust. Bald yellowed patches where sheep had grazed over the summer now stood empty. He could make out a figure on the dusty path leading up over Mynydd Y Gwyddel to Merthyr. A man with two dogs who were clearly enjoying their walk. He suddenly had an urge to be up there on the mountain. Maybe the stillness would clear his mind. And Guinness could do with a walk. He took his coat from the peg in the hall. Even before he got there Guinness was around his feet, yelping madly and throwing herself at his legs.

"Down girl! Wait."

The small black and cream collie-cross sat down, her tail

1

swishing across the carpet. She let out a sorrowful whine. As Rhys reached for her lead she lost her composure completely and danced on her back legs across the hall. Rhys smiled.

"Ok Guinness. Sit."

Guinness tried to obey, but was overcome by excitement. Rhys battled with the clasp on her lead and finally made it through the door with an over eager Guinness barking her delight to the rest of the street. She ran back and forth, wrapping the lead around Rhys' legs.

"Guinness, what are you doing? Silly dog.."

He patted the dog's head, disentangled himself from the lead and pressed the catch to shorten it to a more manageable length. Then man and dog proceeded in a more dignified fashion to the woods at the bottom of the mountain. The estate had been built on the site of an old farm. Some of the houses were actually in the woodlands along the wide dirt track that led up the mountain. Rhys had often wondered about their history. They were old, but fine large houses, nothing like the tiny miner's cottages which snaked up the other side of the mountain towards the now disused colliery site. All that remained from the once thriving iron and coal industry of a hundred years previous was the old railway line. It ran horizontally from the old colliery along the bottom edge of the farm cutting a sharp straight line across the mountain. Another track crossed it vertically, going up and over the mountain into what was once the seething human misery of the Merthyr Ironworks.

Rhys knew all of this by heart. He was a history student. He had planned to become a history teacher, hoping to impart his love of the subject to a future generation of Welsh children. His Teaching Certificate year, however, was beginning to make him think that maybe the future generation had no interest whatsoever in what had gone before. His dreams of retelling

2

the story of "Dic Penderyn and the Merthyr Rising" to spell-bound faces had very much fallen by the wayside.

The air was crisp with the first tinges of autumn frost. No one was around on this Wednesday afternoon. The brook sang and chuckled to itself as it gambolled over stones and pebbles. Birds gossiped noisily in the trees above them. On a branch in front of them a solitary robin stood transfixed keeping Rhys and the dog firmly in its gaze. As they passed, it swept down to retrieve a worm from the hedgerow. They left the main path and began to climb. Rhys could hear vague noises from the golf course below as his feet crunched the frost-crispened earth of the path. Guinness was off the lead now, busily investigating things only of huge interest to dogs, and maybe David Attenborough.

Just three months ago Rhys had thought he had his life sewn up. He had just graduated with a first class honours degree in history, he had a place at the college he wanted and everything seemed to be falling into place. And then, on that fateful day in October, he had gone to a compulsory lecture on "Bullying in Schools" and his world turned upside down.

The college was at the forefront of research into bullying. The lecturer was the "expert in the field" and everyone was expected to do well in this module, so the lecture theatre was packed. He had arrived early and secured a good seat about half way down the hall. There were a few spare seats a little further along the row, where the view was obscured by a large square pillar, but other than that, every seat was taken. Rhys shoved his bag under the seat, found his notebook and settled down. The lecture was just about to start when two girls began pushing past along the row to the spare seats. He stood up to get out of the way. The second of the girls caught her foot in the strap of his bag and almost fell flat on her face. Rhys apologised and tried to reach down to disentangle her, but he was trapped between the seat and the girl. He caught the aroma of vanilla as her dark hair brushed against his face. She edged past, dragging his bag from under the seat, with the strap still caught around her ankle and sat down. Rhys stared in disbelief. She lifted a slim leg skyward and retrieved the bag. He was aware that his mouth was open and that the muscles to close it didn't seem to be working. He caught her eye and she flashed him a warm smile as she mouthed "sorry!" and passed his bag along the line back to him. There was much giggling around him and he could feel the heat travelling up his neck. He was sure he was beetroot red. He was still staring at her, but she was taking notes now. The lecture had begun and Rhys hadn't even noticed. This was not good.

The lecture finished. Rhys looked at his notes in disgust. The only legible thing on the page was "ASK HER OUT" in capital letters at the side of the page. Right. He would. But she was gorgeous and he was, well, him. He glanced across the row to where she had been sitting. She was already on her feet and heading out of the room. His stomach did somersaults. For one insane moment he actually thought he could do it and he got to his feet. Then he caught sight of a tall blonde boy talking to her and his courage departed. He watched her walk through the open doors at the back of the hall. She was gone. And so was his chance.

He muttered to himself as he left the room. Who was he trying to kid? She was lovely. She probably already had a boyfriend. And if she didn't there were bound to be dozens of guys lined up. What did he think he was going to say to her anyway?

"Hi. I'm the guy whose bag nearly upended you." Yeah right. That would sound good. Or how about "I'm the plonker who couldn't close his mouth for staring at you."

Rhys shrugged, checked his watch and headed for his next tutorial.

Chips with Everything

❧ ❧

It had been a long morning. Their tutor had spent the last two hours wittering on about the "noun clause". It was a speech they had heard many times before. It was the session John Jenkins always gave when he hadn't prepared anything. He was famous right throughout the department for it. Elen and Rhian had counted the tiles on the ceiling, the dots on the carpet, anything to stop themselves from falling asleep. Now they were making their way into the refectory to grab a well earned sandwich.

"Can you believe that man? To think I got out of bed at ten past eight to listen to that!"

Rhian Evans made a face. Her friend laughed.

"Rhian. I picked you up at twenty past! Don't tell me you didn't get up till ten past."

Rhian shrugged.

"You better believe it."

Elen and Rhian had been friends since infant school. You could always rely on Rhian to make you laugh. She was a large girl – not so much in physical size but in her sheer presence. Rhian did everything loudly. She was forever getting herself into embarrassing situations, usually with boys, and it was usually left to Elen to get her out of them. Even now, she was tossing her black curls and flashing her eyes at a worried looking guy in the food queue. Elen knew it was just so that she could push into the line, but the poor victim wasn't aware of that.

They were both in their final year of a B.Ed in Primary Education. Elen had always wanted to be a teacher. She wasn't sure what Rhian wanted. Rhian never had much of a mind of her own about things like that, and tended to hang on to Elen's skirts. When she announced that she was going to go to the same college to study the same thing, Elen was a little annoyed at first. But then she thought that the company would be nice. At least she wouldn't be in a strange place on her own. They both lived at home and travelled to the college every day. Well, that was the theory. In practice they both ended up staying with friends quite often. And in Rhian's case they were quite often friends she hadn't met until half an hour before.

The refectory was full. As usual. A group of burly sports science students pushed passed the girls and into the long queue for food.

Elen sighed.

"Manners of a herd of wildebeest. Do you want a coffee? I'm not sure I can be bothered to queue."

Rhian looked resigned.

"I'm going to have to. I didn't bring sandwiches. Think I'll go for a jacket potato with cheese. You look for somewhere to sit."

Elen surveyed the room. Every seat appeared to be taken.

"Look there's one."

"Where?"

"Over there by the window."

Rhian pointed to the far side of the room.

"Hey look" she added with a grin

"It's Bag Boy!"

Elen looked and sure enough Rhian was right. There was

the boy whose bag had very nearly broken her ankle a couple of weeks before. Rhian had really pulled Elen's leg about him.

"He fancies you, I know he does. He went scarlet. Right down to his boots! And the way he sat there with his mouth open!"

Elen was not so sure.

"He was embarrassed for me that's all. I did make something of a pantomime of it, now didn't I? And anyway, we wouldn't have had to sit behind the pillar if you hadn't overslept. Again."

Elen surveyed the room again. No, the only seat in the hall seemed to be next to Bag Boy and his friends. Nothing for it. She would have to sit there.

"Hi. Did your bag survive my onslaught?"

Rhys looked up. His mouth went dry. Oh, god, what was he going to say? He heard his voice muttering

"Yeah, sure. No problems."

He sounded like an idiot. He had been hoping to bump into her for the last two weeks and now here she was and his brain had picked this particular moment to go on holiday.

"Is it ok if my friend and I sit here?"

Rhys nodded. He didn't trust his mouth to reply. Friend? He wondered if the friend was male or female. Then he caught sight of Rhian gesticulating in the queue. He gave an involuntary shudder. There was something about that girl that scared the living daylights out of him.

"I think your friend is trying to get your attention."

Elen turned to look. She smiled sweetly at Rhys.

"Will you keep the seats for us please? She's probably just realised she hasn't got any money. Again."

Rhys nodded blindly. Elen dumped her bag on the seat beside him and went to Rhian's aid.

Rhys stared after her. Then stared at the luggage on the seat next to him. A large turquoise suede bag with a pink key ring attached to the zip. There was something printed on the key fob. He strained to read it, trying to look as casual as possible. Elen was now paying Rhian's bill, so Rhys took a chance and leant over to get a better look at the fob.

"Elen" it read, in purple lettering with silver outlines. At least now, he knew her name.

The girls came over and sat down. Elen opened her sandwiches, Rhian was tucking in noisily to curry and chips.

"What happened to your jacket potato?" enquired Rhian.

"It went out of the window when I smelt the curry. Do you want some? It's lush!"

There were three things Rhian could rarely say "No" to; men, food and alcohol. The latter two particularly if someone else was paying, and the former when she had consumed a surfeit of the latter! Rhian's judgement on the attractiveness and suitability of men waned considerably as the night progressed. Elen had dragged her out of more than one club protesting violently as she was bundled into a taxi that she had just met the love of her life. Elen was much more cautious. She liked to get to know someone very well before agreeing to go out with them. The trouble was, most men didn't seem to want to take the time to do that.

She studied Rhys out of the corner of her eye. He wasn't at all bad looking. Dark, tightly curled hair, soft unbelievably blue eyes. Really long eyelashes. She pulled herself up short. This was taking in far too much information. She really ought to find out more about "Bag Boy". She stretched out her hand.

"We haven't really introduced ourselves. Elen Lloyd"

Rhys put down his bacon roll and wiped his hand on his trousers. He looked at his hand.

"Err, I don't think I had better shake hands. Still a bit greasy. Rhys Harris."

He was about to continue but Rhian was not about to be left out.

"I'm Rhian. We're doing Primary, Welsh Medium. What course are you doing?"

"PGCE Secondary. History."

There was a long pause. Rhys struggled for something to say. Nothing he rehearsed in his head seemed to sound right. It was Elen who broke the silence.

"Where are you doing your teaching prac?"

Rhys looked at her gratefully.

"I've done some observations but I haven't started my teaching block yet. We get to know the schools we will be teaching at tomorrow. I'm hoping mine will be in the valleys, rather than Cardiff."

"Are you from the Valleys then? We are from the Rhondda."

"Are you? Great. I'm from Aberdare."

Rhys couldn't think of anything more to say.

Rhian could though.

"Cardiff people aren't the same as Valleys people are they? You know where you are with valleys kids. What you see is what you get."

"It's not so much that – it's the travelling. It takes an age to get here by 9.15 – if I had to get to a school in Cardiff by 8.30 I would have to leave by half seven at the latest. At least it doesn't take so long to get over to the next valley."

Just as Rhys thought he was beginning to relax he felt a tug on his sleeve.

"Come on, Rhysey boy, we've got the dragon next. And you don't want to be late for her tutorial now do you? You going to introduce me then?"

A lively looking sandy haired youth was urging Rhys to hurry.

"Erm, Elen and Rhian this is Splodge. Erm, Simon."

"How dos. Rhys, come on, we have got to move it."

Splodge nodded. Rhian's pupils dilated visibly.

"Splodge?" she enquired?

He grinned.

"Simon Paul Lodge. It sort of stuck."

Then the boys hot footed it out of the refectory and up the stairs.

"He was nice" murmured Rhian.

"Yes. I thought so too" agreed Elen.

"I didn't think you went for gingas."

"What do you mean, ginger? His hair was almost black…." Elen stopped herself. "Oh, you meant…"

"Splodge" nodded Rhian.

Then they both burst out laughing.

The Emperor

෨ ෧

Carla Theodoro picked up the phone in the well lit orderly office. This was her domain and she kept it the way that she liked it, tidy, organised, everything in its place — although this was not an easy task with a boss like Giovanni Maconi. He stored everything in his head and gave out information on a "need to know" basis. Carla sometimes wondered if he trusted anyone at all.

"Mr Maconi's office."

She recognised the voice on the phone at once and sighed silently to herself. This was not going to put her boss in a good mood.

"Yes, Signora Maconi, I have given him the message. He is still in a meeting at the moment. I will remind him as soon as he comes out. Yes, of course I will. Thank you Signora Maconi."

This was the fourth time she had rung that day to remind her husband that it was their eldest son's birthday party at four o'clock that afternoon. Carla looked at her watch. 3.15. What were the chances of him making it on time, she wondered? Probably nil, but then he hardly ever made it to any of his family's birthdays on time. Vittorio was eleven that day. His eldest son. Carla had picked out the present for him, wrapped it and chosen the card for his father to sign. She suspected it was still in the boot of his car. So strange that a man with a mind as sharp as a razor when it came to business became so absent minded when it came to his family.

The office door opened. Two men emerged and the contrast between them could not have been more striking. The American was the taller, larger and should have been more imposing in his sharply pressed suit, but this was not so. He was sweating from more than the Milan heat. The Italian looked ice cool by comparison, sleek Armani suit, soft caramel coloured leather shoes, every inch in control, as calculating as a cat.

"You drive a hard bargain, Mac" the American shook his head and gave an over-forced laugh.

"That's what they pay me for, Todd. Giorgio and I will draw up the contracts. Carla will have them sent over to you by courier tomorrow. A pleasure doing business with you."

They shook hands. Carla noticed that the American didn't meet her boss's eye. Yet again another supposed "hard nut" had cracked before him. Carla didn't know the terms of the agreement but she was sure Todd Wilson had been forced to cut profits to a margin in order to meet Mac's terms.

She nodded and escorted him out of the office and into the corridor to the lift.

"That boss of yours is some tough cookie."

"Mr Maconi is one of the best, Sir."

"Sure is. You know they call him "the ice man"? They say no-one has ever made him break out into a sweat! I can certainly believe that."

Carla smiled.

"I will have the contracts with you in the morning Mr Wilson."

The tall American looked at her quizzically. She knew what he was thinking. How did a perfectly pleasant girl like her cope with working for such an unfeeling creature as "Mac"

Maconi? She wondered the same thing herself at least twenty times a week. It paid the rent, and the rest she didn't risk her conscience thinking about.

She had worked for S-Systems Telecommunications for nine years. Back then they had been a small player in the field, but things had taken off with the advent of Bluetooth technology and thanks to some shrewd deals the firm was now on the cusp of becoming a major player. The deal Mac had just broached with Todd Wilson would give them an even bigger share of the market. For a second, she wondered how many people would lose their jobs as a result, or how many jobs would be "off-shored" to save costs. Then she put it out of her mind. If it wasn't S-Systems it would be someone else. There were too many telecoms companies in Europe and the next twelve months would see which ones stayed and which ones went to the wall. In a way, many of them owed their jobs to the tough negotiating skills of "Mac – the ice man Maconi".

She closed the door behind her. Through the open door she could see Mac already e-mailing the details through to his boss.

"Carla, can we have some coffee in here. Giorgio and I are going to be here for the duration"

Carla was tight lipped.

"Signora Maconi rang, Sir, to remind you about Vittorio's party today."

Mac frowned.

"What time?"

"Four o'clock."

"No can do Carla. No can do. Giorgio and I have to amend the contracts and get them proofed by the morning. Ring Kata and tell her I'm going to be late."

With that his head went back down to his work. Further discussion was out of the question. Carla picked up the phone to ring Mrs Maconi. This was one call she really was not looking forward to making.

"Signora Maconi? Yes, it's Carla. Yes, I gave him the message. He has been unavoidably detained – a very important client. He will be along as soon as he can. I really couldn't say, Signora Maconi. He is in a meeting at present. No, I can't do that. He has asked specifically not to be disturbed. Yes, I do understand. Yes, I will tell him. Yes, I'm writing that down. Thank you Signora Maconi."

The phone slammed down at the other end of the line. Carla held the receiver away from her ear and looked at the scribbled note she had just taken. Mac would need all of his negotiating skills to get out of this one.

Family Matters

❧ ❧

It was some time after seven o'clock when Mac pulled up outside his home on the outskirts of Milan. He reached into the glove compartment, took out a small leather pouch emptying its contents into his hand and slipping the gold band onto his finger. He took a breath and stretched his shoulders. It had been a long, if profitable day. Now he had to change his mind-set to family mode. He picked up his briefcase and locked the car. The evening heat hit his body. He loosened his tie.

Mac put his key in the lock and met his wife's icy stare as she opened the door.

"The party is over; your son is playing pool with his friends. Vittorio, remember? The son you had eleven years ago."

"Kata, it couldn't be helped. You know how the market is at the moment. I have to take every chance I can. You want a secure future for them, don't you? Look at your brother. No job, no house. Is that what you want?"

Mac was calculating. He knew he had just lit the blue touch paper. Attack was the best means of defence. Kata glared at him and slammed down the cup she was holding onto the table. Her eyes were flashing now. Steel blue. Kata in a rage was truly a thing of beauty. Mac thought that sometimes he provoked her just to watch, fascinated. It was like watching a

15

storm, lightning flashing across the night sky. Powerful. Evocative. A being so alive.

"Don't you dare throw my brother at me Mac Maconi! Bjorn is a good man. They may well be living with my mother but he would never be too busy for his son's birthday."

She stormed out, long blond hair swishing as she went. Mac watched her and smiled. Kata was the only person who ever won an argument with him. She was a challenge.

They had been married for almost twelve years. She was an ex-model and still very lovely. Her long blonde hair, a legacy from her Swedish mother, cascading over her shoulders. Her even longer legs, slim, toned. Just the thought still made him weak. They had two children. Fine Italian boys. Dark eyed. Olive skinned. Vittorio, the eldest had his mother's light hair, Orlando was more like Mac, well, physically at least. Black curls falling over even darker eyes. They were both settled happily at school in Milan. Vittorio at eleven, was tall for his age. A lover of football and already noticing the ladies. Orlando was nine. A dreamer. His head was always in a book.

Mac picked up the package Carla had given him and headed for the pool room. Vittorio looked up. Mac could see the hurt in his eyes but he brushed it aside.

"Vitto, I'm so sorry I'm late. Big business meeting. This yank kept me talking for hours. But no talk of business now – what do I have for my favourite son?"

Vittorio shrugged. Mac waved the box in front of him.

"What does every boy in your class want I wonder?"

Vittorio's eyes followed the box. He was so angry with his father for missing yet another birthday. But he wanted what was in the box. Mac was gambling on this. He knew his eldest son – he was too much like himself.

"Ah, you don't want it. Maybe Orlando wants it? What do

16

you think, Orlando? Is the very latest games console too old for a nine year old?"

Vittorio grabbed the box from in front of his brother's arms. He pulled off the paper.

"Wow! Where did you get it? I thought they weren't available in Europe yet."

"I had it flown over especially for you. It pays to have contacts, eh? Nothing is too good for my son's birthday!"

Mac put an arm around Vittorio's shoulder. Out of the corner of his eye he caught sight of Kata watching coldly. She came towards him and whispered in his ear as she passed.

"Except his father being here on time."

"Right" beamed Mac, as though he hadn't heard. "Who wants to go try this beast out then? Vitto, shall we set it up?"

The boys all crowded round as Mac held court plugging the machine in and displaying the games Carla had chosen.

Kata stood at the door. Her eyes betrayed no emotion. Mac went over to her.

"I think that went well."

"You are lucky Carla has her finger on the pulse of an eleven year old." Kata was curt.

"Carla? No no. What would she know about boys? Come on, Kata, you don't think I would ask my secretary to choose my own son's present now do you?"

Kata softened.

She handed him a cup of coffee.

"Have you eaten?"

"Not yet. I was in meetings until late. It was a choice between food and not getting here until midnight. See, I do have my priorities right."

His eyes met hers.

Kata stared into those bottomless brown eyes. She wondered if he was telling the truth. She was angry with him and something told her that she was being manipulated. Never the less there was a topic she wanted to broach and she sensed he was in a mood to appease.

"I saw Amanda today."

Mac bristled. Amanda was Kata's former agent from her modelling days.

"And?"

"She has some work for me. Catalogue stuff. For ladies who lunch."

"Kata, I thought I had made myself clear on this."

"You did. And so did I. I'm bored Mac. The boys are at school all day, you are at work. I need a career again."

"You need a career? You have a career. You are a wife, you are a mother. What career is more important than that? The boys need you."

"This won't affect the boys."

"How can it not affect them? How are they going to feel to see their mother half naked in magazines? Their friends at school leering and saying things boys should never hear about their mothers?"

Kata was cold. "Mac, we are talking about hands and feet here. I'm too old for fashion stuff. And anyway, I have never appeared half naked."

The curtain of white blonde hair flicked angrily across her face.

"Ah come on Kata. Those sheer dresses. You could see everything."

The memory of seeing his then girlfriend in those seductive outfits in glossy magazines was still fresh. How the other guys envied him. But even then, part of Mac felt that she should only dress like that for him. Yet it was a thrill, somehow, that other men were allowed to see parts of her that only he was allowed to touch.

18

"Mac you are exaggerating. And this is nothing like that."
She stared, ice blue eyes holding his gaze.

"I won't have it Kata. Think of my position. How can I be taken seriously if my wife is on display in a cheap catalogue? It could jeopardise everything I have worked for. We agreed on this before we married, remember? "

Kata was silent. Yes, they had agreed. Mac had even made her agree in writing. But she had never really thought that he meant it. How could he ask her to permanently give up her career? It was different when the boys were younger. She looked for some sort of softening in his eyes. There was none. He was not going to give way.

"You do see my point? You have a role. When I get my promotion you won't have time to work anyway. You will be one of the 'ladies who lunch'."

Kata looked at the floor.

"You win again" she said softly.

He lifted her chin and looked into her eyes.

"It isn't about winning."

"Isn't it?"

Mac ignored her comment and kissed her cheek.

"How would you like to go over to Brenzone for the weekend? The contracts should be in tomorrow. I don't foresee any hiccups. If you go up in the morning I can join you tomorrow night."

She brightened.

"The boys have school."

"One day won't hurt. Come on, it would be good to spend time together. And the boys haven't seen Bibi for ages. What do you say?"

"Yes. It would be good. We could do with a break."

The Quest

❧   ❧

Rhys blinked as he walked into the half light of the pub. He cast his eyes around and then ordered a coke for himself and a pint of Dark for Splodge.

"Thanks."

Splodge took a full gulp.

"Well, have you struck lucky yet?"

This was the fourth pub they had been to that night and it was only ten o'clock. At this rate Rhys would be broke by stop tap and if Splodge was true to his usual form he would end up being sick out of the car window. It had been his idea to go on a pub crawl to find the two girls they had been talking to the other day. He said he was sick of Rhys wandering around like a moon struck calf. Rhys had protested that if it was meant to be then they would bump into each other again.

"Sod destiny. If you fancy her, go get her. Are you a man or a mouse Emrys Harris? No, don't answer that. I can hear you squeaking from here."

Only Rhys' mother ever called him by his full name. And then only when she was really angry with him. The truth was, Rhys was terrified of meeting Elen again. He really liked her. Trouble was, whenever she came into view the connections from his brain to his mouth seemed to short circuit and all that came out was sheer gobbledygook.

Rhys took a sip of his coke. His eyes scanned the room. It looked as if they had drawn a blank again.

Then, from around a corner came a hearty forced laugh. Rhys shuddered. Could it be? He moved further along the bar to get a better look. Rhian spotted him before he spotted her. And she also clocked Splodge. In seconds she was swaying towards them, make-up already showing signs of wear, her eyes bright with alcoholic glaze.

"Hello boys." She giggled. Her ample bosom bounced before them swathed in too tight pink Lycra.

"Come and join us."

Before either of them could protest she had dragged Splodge half way across the room and towards a group of girls clearly celebrating a hen night. An older woman was wearing a bride's veil and sporting L plates.

"This is my mam. She's getting married" Rhian informed them proudly.

"Congratulations" ventured Rhys.

Rhian still had Splodge by the hand.

"Mam, this is Splodge. Splodge say hello to my mammy."

Splodge extended his free hand. Rhian still had a grip of iron on the other one. Mammy was clearly sossled.

"Pleashed to meet you Splish"

She shook his hand too vigorously. Splodge finally extricated himself and looked around for a spare seat. Elen was sitting in the far corner of the group. Rhys stood rooted to the spot. He so wanted to go over and make small talk but his fight or flight mechanisms had gone all wonky. He flattened himself against the wall. She was talking to one of the other girls and hadn't seen him yet. She wore an ivory coloured halter neck top which hugged her slim figure. Rhys noted the smooth curve of her shoulders and the way her mouth turned up at the corners when she laughed. She must have sensed him watching her as she suddenly glanced his way. Rhys was mortified as her eyes met his. He was transfixed, like a rabbit in headlights, not knowing whether to look away, or wave or run.

Rhian came to his rescue. She had reluctantly let go of Splodge when he protested that he simply had to answer the call of nature. Rhys now had to meet Mammy. Rhian insisted. Just as the ordeal was about to begin Elen tapped him on the shoulder.

"There's a spare seat in the corner. Kathy's leaving now."

The said Kathy was, indeed putting on her coat. Gratefully Rhys let go of Mammy's clammy hand and squeezed past the table to the seat in the corner. There wasn't much room. Kathy was much smaller than Rhys. He perched himself awkwardly on the edge of the seat and tried not to smash his knees against the table. Rhian sat next to him. Rhys wriggled backwards to try to make more room.

"It's a bit squashed in here" she said.

"Just a bit. Would you like a drink?"

"I'm fine thanks." She indicated the full glass in front of her.

"You driving?"

"What?" Rhys looked blank.

"The coke?"

"Oh. Yes. And someone has to keep and eye on Splodge." He noticed that she was drinking orange juice.

"Are you driving too?"

She smiled.

"Not tonight. We have booked a mini bus. There's no way I'm having a drunken Rhian's mam in my car. Look at her. She's hardly got a leg under her."

"Like mother like daughter." The words were out of Rhys' mouth before he could stop himself.

Rhian laughed out loud.

"You can say that again! They aren't safe to be let loose out on the town, either of them. I hope the mothers of Cardiff have locked up their sons."

"I think Splodge is a condemned man" Rhys was laughing in spite of himself.

"Oh crikey. Look!"

Rhian jerked her hand towards the centre of the room. Both Rhian and her Mammy had their arms draped around Splodge and the three of them were teetering unevenly to the strains of "Viva Espania". Splodge's arms were waving above his head in a gesture that could have been either enthusiasm or drowning.

"I think I had better rescue him" he stammered.

"What, and risk the wrath of a rejected Rhian and the might of her amorous mother? I think not! Unless you are a very brave man indeed Rhys Harris."

Rhys had already got to his feet, committed now to the action.

At this point there was a commotion on the dance floor. Mammy had fallen over and was lying on her back with one red stilettoed foot pointing at the ceiling. Splodge took the opportunity to retreat to the bar. Rhian was now helping Mammy to her feet with the help of several other girls. Elen was chatting to the girl sitting next to her. Rhys stood glass in hand at the edge of the dance floor wondering what to do. Elen was lost in conversation. He had lost his seat to one of the other girls, who had taken the opportunity to sit as soon as the seat became vacant. He walked back to the bar and stood next to Splodge.

"Well? It looked as if you were in there."

"What? No. Just making conversation. I don't think she's interested."

Rhys was subdued. Splodge ordered another pint, and a

half for Rhys. The girls were now putting on their coats and heading out of the room. Splodge wiped the froth from the pint off his upper lip.

"Do you want to go in pursuit or what? If you do, you can keep that pair of man eaters away from me. It was like being in a sauna in there."

"No. Leave it."

Rhys watched Elen walk through the door of the pub. He hadn't even asked where they were going next. For a second he thought about following them. Then he realised that would just look totally pathetic. He stared mournfully at the bottom of his glass and kicked himself for blowing it. Again.

Homecoming

      ↝   ↜

Summer was melting into autumn as Mac drove onto the road which would take him home. The trees on the lakeside were already beginning to get tinged with yellow and brown. The tourists hadn't gone home yet. The car ground to a halt as he reached Riva. Tyres squealing, horns sounding. He had forgotten the noisy gridlock of his home. In London, or Milan these sounds would have been frustrating. Here, just kilometres from the town where he was born, they were comforting.

Echoes of his childhood. Papa waving his arms out of the window and shouting. Mama saying it made no difference. Mac and his brothers straining to see the lake.

It was his grandmother's house. He had spent most of his summers there as a child. She still lived there, on her own. Mac's parents had died many years since – his father from cirrhosis of the liver, his mother, from a broken heart. He and his brothers used the house as a holiday retreat now. Mac arranged for a local girl to keep the place clean and to take care of his independent grandmother. She was from Spanish gypsy stock. "Bibi" he had always called her. As a small child he couldn't pronounce her Romani name. His cousins called her "Bibi" – Romani for aunt, so Mac followed suit. "Bibi" she was and "Bibi" she remained. She was "Daći dej" to his brothers but although she had seventeen grandchildren, Mac was her favourite. She idolised him. And he, her. She was the one person on the planet that he truly cared about.

Even when he was child she seemed ancient, her skin the colour of leather, her clothes always brightly coloured and her silver curls falling into her eyes. She smelt of herbs – basil and lavender. Although she was now in her eighties, her eyes were still so alive. She knew more than anyone could tell. He smiled to himself, knowing that before he did anything else he would have to take a cup of tea and Bibi would not settle until she had read the leaves. His grandmother did not approve of his marriage to Kata.

"It's not good, Gio, to marry someone you do not love." She had told him.

"But I do love her" he had protested.

Bibi had tilted her head and looked him straight in the eye.

"Do you? I think not. You will break her heart, *chajoko chavo* (grandson). Yes. Then she will break yours."

He told himself that he took it all with a pinch of salt – but that didn't stop him carrying the talisman she had given him as a child in his pocket. She was full of dreams. Always telling him that he was meant for greatness – that he was descended from one of the emperors of ancient Rome. Which one, he had no idea. He allowed her fantasies. Giovanni Maconi, he told himself, lived in the real world. There was no room there for childish thoughts or flights of fancy. He was his own man. But she did hold a special place in his heart. She was so devoted to him that even he could not help but return her love. She was becoming frail. He didn't like to think about that too much. She would be pleased to see him, and more pleased still to learn that the boys were coming up later. Kata did not want them to miss school, so she had decided to drive up tomorrow. Mac had finished work uncharacteristically early. He wanted some time with his grandmother. There were things he could only discuss with her.

Slowly the road wound its way around the lake. Settlements clung desperately to the mountainside. The monastery with its pink roof came into view on the other side of the lake. In Limone over tanned, over thin women would be picking their way along the shoreline shops, pausing to take in the latest from Gucci. The sun worshipers were still out in force, even though the Angelus bells would soon be ringing. On the shingle stony faced thirty something women lay on towels in the tiniest of thongs. Any other day and he would have slowed down for a better look. He took in with amusement the crowd of teenage boys, their floral shorts flapping around their knees, flicking their tousled locks out of dangerous looking eyes and trying too hard not to be seen staring at the naked breasts on show just metres away from them. One of the beauties got up and shook her towel. There was a splash as an open-mouthed youth fell off the jetty and into the water. Laughter at his protests. Even the tawny skinned lovely who had caused the calamity smiled. The power of women.

The soft evening sunshine made him sleepy. The bells were ringing, calling the faithful to prayer. Perhaps he would go. Yes, why not? He left the main road and started to climb uphill towards the church. Mac had forgotten how narrow and winding the roads were here. All these blind bends. He was out of practice after living in the city for so long.

It came from nowhere.

"What the…"

A lorry was heading towards him on the wrong side of the road.

"Where did he come from…?"

There was nowhere to go. The road was too narrow and it was a sheer drop on his side. Slowly, so very slowly the side of the truck approached his car. It hit the front of the vehicle and seemed to bounce. The sound of metal grating against metal. The smell of burning rubber.

The car began to turn over in slow motion. Mac's head went forward, then back again, then jerked forward once more, hitting the steering wheel. The horn sounded.

Black.

Strange Events

❧ ❧

Mac was driving along a wide road at the bottom of a flat broad valley. There were trees on the hillsides. Pines. He could smell them. He must be getting closer to the mountains. He could see the river to his left, winding its lazy way along. He was climbing steadily. The road seemed to be tracing the river back to its source. There was nothing else to do that day, so he might as well follow it and see where it led him.

The road really began to climb now. Twisting from side to side with hairpin bends that made the Monte Carlo rally look like the M1. Up and up. Mac thought that he really should have brought the 4 x 4. The mountain fell away to his left in an almost sheer drop. Houses looked like toys on the other side of the valley. Sheep grazed like wisps of cotton wool. Waterfalls glinted in the late evening sun.

The air was getting thinner. Where was he? This mountain seemed higher than any of the Dolomites. Still the road led him up. There were no houses now. The ground to each side was barren. Snow frosted the steep sides of the valley. Even the car seemed to make no sound.

It was so cold. Mac's breath came out in clouds before him. He was almost at the summit.

At the top he could see a great open plateau to one side. It stretched out as far as the eye could see, verdant plains filled with grapes, corn and apples. On the other side the mountain fell down steeply with a great river rushing down to meet the sea. Mac left the car and began following the river down stream. It had been a while since he had walked anywhere. His muscles ached. His feet hurt as he stumbled over rocks. The sound of the river was deafening. It was becoming less steep now.

There was a small boat tied up at the side of the river. An old man stood beside the boat. Old! He was as aged as Methuselah. His olive face was creased into a thousand lines around an almost toothless mouth. His clothes were so dusty it was impossible to say what he was wearing.

Mac raised his hand in greeting.

The boatman smiled. A single toothed grin. Then he placed the rope from the boat into Mac's hand and walked away. Mac looked at the boat. He turned to speak to the ancient boatman, but he was nowhere to be seen.

Mac got into the boat and let it take him downstream.

It was so peaceful. The birds were calling to each other. Fish leapt in the river. The water was so clear that Mac thought that if he put out his hand he could catch one.

The river widened now. Bigger boats passed him. Ocean going boats. He could see a vast city on the shoreline. Where was he? Venice? No, he didn't recognise any of it. He tied up the boat at the riverbank and walked towards the city. Before him was a huge mansion, like an ancient Roman villa. It was completely deserted. He walked through the courtyard through a corridor, into another courtyard, then another.

He was facing a harbour. In the harbour was a flotilla of yachts.

Anchored in the centre was an absolute beauty of a craft. All white, with gold and silver trimmings. Very nice. Mac walked towards it to have a better look. His feet were on something cool. Marble. There was a marble bridge leading down to the boat. Funny. He hadn't noticed that before. The bridge led right on to the boat itself. He looked around for someone to ask "permission to come aboard" but there was no one. The boat, the harbour, the city. All were deserted.

No sooner had his feet touched the deck than they were underway. The sail was hoisted by unseen hands and they were travelling fast. Over a deep blue ocean. He felt tired. His eyes closed and he drifted in and out of sleep.

Mac had no idea how long he slept for. It could have been days, or even weeks. When he came to, they were anchoring on a pretty island. A tall red haired man waved to him from the shore. Mac got his land legs together and walked towards him. He motioned Mac towards an immaculate looking Lear jet. Silently Mac was led on board. He sat down, questioning nothing.

The jet soared over green rolling valleys and tall mountains. Mac saw rivers, castles, farms. He surveyed the island from end to end. Then the plane set down near a wood. There were birch, ash and oak trees. A path led clearly to a courtyard.

Mac followed the path and beheld the most amazing castle he had ever seen. It was like something out of a fairy tale. Tiny, but with red-ish walls and tiled, round towers, quite unlike the square walled citadels of his homeland. Inside, there was gilt and splendour everywhere. He could see a room ahead of him covered with paintings. There were butterflies around the door. Birds on the walls and on the ceiling.

Two auburn haired youths rushed past him, playing with a ball. It almost felt as though they walked through him. Mac entered the room. Opposite him, in a very ornate chair, sat an old man with grey hair. He was pointing at something with a small boy at his side. The boy ran over to the other side of the room. There stood a young woman dressed in jeans and

T-shirt. She was stunning. Mac couldn't take his eyes off her, and yet there was something about her beauty that was almost painful.

The boy took her by the hand and pulled her to the centre of the room to see a painting. He was pointing to a figure dressed in white. A beautiful woman. It looked just like her. Beside her was a knight in medieval costume, kneeling. Mac knew his face. With a shock, he realised that it was his face. The knight was himself.

Mac could barely look at the girl, for she took his breath away. She turned towards him and smiled. He felt his feet moving towards her, or was it the room that was spinning. The wooden floor was uneven. He saw her stumble and stretched out his arms to catch her fall. She was like gossamer in his arms. Sweet perfume clouded his head. Her face looked up at his. His hand cradled the smallness of her waist. He could feel the softness of her cheek and the warmth of her breath on his face.

Mac turned his face towards her and closed his eyes to kiss her. Before her lips could brush his, he heard the sound of shouting.

A shrill noise. Some sort of alarm. Someone shouted "Stand clear". Lights. Such bright lights.

Mac's hands were limp at his sides. He forced his eyes to open.

All around him were people in green gowns and masks. Mac knew this place. Where was he? Then it dawned on him. Hospital. He was in a hospital. Where was the girl? His arms were empty. Every bone in his body felt bruised. He was fighting for breath. It felt like there was something in his throat. His stomach hurt. Everything hurt. He was wracked with pain beyond belief. But the anguish in his heart for the girl in his dreams outweighed all of these.

The Morning After

❧ ❦

Elen sounded her horn for the second time. She looked at her watch. It was 8.15 on a dreary Monday morning. The traffic was always worse on Mondays. Everyone always slept that little bit later and left it just that fraction too late to start out for work. So everyone was a little bit bad tempered, or half asleep, or both. She hated driving to college on Mondays.

Where was Rhian? She got out of her car and walked across to the row of pebble dashed terraced houses. The lights were on in Rhian's house, she could discern vague shapes moving behind the frosted glass of the front door. She rang the doorbell. Peter, Rhian's future step father answered it.

"Oh. Morning, Elen. Or should I say '*Bore da*'". He smiled weakly.

"Is Rhian about? We are late already."

He looked perplexed.

"Oh. I think she's surfaced. I heard someone moving about upstairs. I haven't seen much of either of them since the hen night on Saturday. They haven't been too well…"

"You don't say?"

Elen raised an eyebrow. She remembered almost pouring Rhian and her mother out of the minibus on the way home. Rhian's mother insisting on hugging her.

"I'm sho glad you are Rhian's friend. I shink of you as a

daughter you know. Ever shince your mam died. Rhian is sho lucky. Hash anyone sheen my handbag? I'm shure I had a handbag…"

At this point Rhian had hit her over the head with the handbag, which everyone had been looking for, for at least 10 minutes and which had been discovered hanging from Rhian's mother's shoulder. Thank goodness they had the hen night a full week before the wedding!

Rhian appeared at the door, ashen faced, no make-up with a piece of toast in her hand.
She nodded towards the car as she pushed past Peter.

"You look terrible!"

"Thanks."

"How's your Mam?"

"Worse than me. We didn't get up yesterday. Apart from to go to the loo. This toast tastes like sand paper."

Elen glanced sideways at her friend who was holding on to her seatbelt as they went round the corner and back onto the main road.

"I wouldn't know. I've never eaten sandpaper."

"Very funny"

"Well, at least you both had a good night."

"Did we? I can't remember. Where did we go after we left the pub?"

"On to two clubs in town. Only one wouldn't let us in. They said you and your Mam had had enough to drink."

"They were probably right. My head feels like a herd of elephants are stampeding over it."

"If you will drink like a prop forward then you only have yourself to blame."

"Oh shh. Just because you don't drink. You've got no idea how I feel."

They drove in silence for the next twenty minutes or so.

"Did I dream it or did Bag Boy and the lovely Splodge turn up at some point?"

"They did."

"What happened? Did you get off with him? Did I get off with Splodge? I must have tried surely?"

"Nothing. No, no and yes. So did your mam. I think she had more luck than you did."

"I don't remember any of it. Oh wait a minute? Nah. We couldn't have danced to Viva Espania..."

"Oh yes you did. And the Macarena. And the Birdie Song."

"Good job I don't remember. How come you didn't get off with 'Love's Young Dream' then? I was sure you had him hooked. All you had to do was reel him in."

Elen tossed her head defensively.

"Either he is *unbelievably* shy or he really isn't interested. I dunno. He went over to rescue Splodge when your mam fell on top of him and he didn't come back. The two of them were still at the bar when we left."

"Didn't you tell them where we were going?"

Elen shot her an angry glance.

"That would have looked at bit desperate now wouldn't it?"

"Totty comes to she who flirts. Guys need a bit of encouragement."

"He got encouragement. I called him over to sit by me didn't I? I don't believe in girls chasing blokes. If he's interested he will have to chase me."

"Get the Prima Donna."

"It's not that. You know what it's like. So many blokes just looking for one thing."

"And..?"

"I want more than that. I want to be wooed. I want romance. I want to be swept of my feet."

"Then you had better move to the continent Mrs Valentino. This is rain soaked Wales. The nearest you'll get to romance is a quick snog behind the bus shelter between halves of the rugby game."

Rhian absent mindedly helped herself to Elen's make-up as they turned into the tree lined avenue heading up towards the college.

"I don't believe you Rhian. Somewhere, there just has to be a nice, good looking, sensitive, intelligent, talented bloke."

"There is."

Elen looked at her.

"Johnny Depp is taken though."

Rhian laughed loudly as Elen pulled into the college grounds.

"Look at this. Not a parking space anywhere. We are going to have to park in the mud behind the sports hall again. Could you just *try* to get up on time tomorrow please?"

They got out of the car and unsuccessfully tried to negotiate the mud. It stuck to Elen's boots and squelched as they trod gingerly back to the path.

"There must be a term for a large patch of mud." Elen mused to herself.

"A squelch. What do you think Rhi? A squelch of mud?"

"Oh stop moaning. You're only crotchety because you aren't getting any…..Seriously though Elen..".

Rhian was in philosophical mood. She continued

"If you want a fella you are really going to have to lower your high standards a bit. Guys like that only exist in films."

"Maybe you are right."

Elen felt totally deflated this morning. She had been delighted to see Rhys walk in on Saturday night but quite depressed after he wandered off, without even saying goodnight.

"And another thing.."

"What?"

"Could you lend me a fiver for lunch? I've left my purse in my other bag."

Of Boys and Men

ॐ ॐ

Kata frowned as she handed the phone to her husband.

"It's Giorgio."

"Yes, yes thanks. I'm much better."

She mouthed "No you're not" and shook her head. Mac waved at her to leave the room. Kata pretended not to have noticed and stood leaning on the door frame.

"Tomorrow. Yes, of course. No problem"

Mac's voice was light. His wife glared at him.

"No. I will be back in next week. Doctors? What do doctors know? I'm fine. Great. See you at eleven tomorrow."

He put the phone down and looked at Kata.

"Mac, have you gone completely mad?"

Kata was fuming.

"It's only ten days since the accident and you are actually thinking of working tomorrow? Doctor Basini said at least a month."

Mac's face betrayed no expression. "Relax. It's just some contracts Giorgio wants me to look at. He is coming here."

Kata tried to read his face.

"No work, Mac. You promised. Not until you are better."

"I am better. Work is just what I need to get over all of this."

What he didn't add was that Carla had already told him that

38

the job he had been pushing for had just come up for grabs. Mac needed to be in the right place at the right time and it was important that he showed no weakness now.

Kata paused. "Did you say he was coming here at eleven? I am taking my mother to the hospital tomorrow morning. Had you forgotten?"

"What? Oh sorry. It slipped my mind. No matter. It's just a few contracts. Nothing taxing. I will be fine."

"I see."

She turned to walk into the kitchen.

"Mac?"

"Yes?"

"Don't push yourself. Please."

Mac smiled.

"Come here."

Kata ran to him and buried her face in his chest.

"You are precious to me. I don't want anything to happen to you. After the accident... I was so scared."

Mac stroked her hair.

"Silly girl. Nothing is going to happen to me. I lead a charmed life."

"It doesn't matter you know. You don't have to keep doing this."

Salt water was making its way down her immaculately made up face.

"Doing what?"

"Proving yourself."

Mac sighed and stared at the ceiling.

"A man has to provide for his children."

"But he doesn't have to kill himself doing it."

Kata swallowed. "Mac, you aren't your father. You don't have to prove that to anyone."

"My father was a lazy good for nothing and my mother had

39

to scrub floors to feed her children. Is that what you mean?"

Mac's voice was ice cold.

"You know what I mean. You have done enough. You don't have to keep driving yourself to get to the top. We are comfortable. We don't need more."

"I need more. I know, somehow, that I'm going to really make it big someday. I'm going to be someone. I have to do whatever it takes. Otherwise – what's the point? Anyone can just exist. I have to do this."

Kata lifted her head and walked out of the room. When he was sure she was out of earshot Mac picked up the phone.

"Carla? Mac. I want you to bring Giorgio here tomorrow. Ok?"

His eyes watched like a cat's for the return of his wife. Ears pricked. He was totally focused.

"Get him here at 10.45. Yes, I know I said eleven. Just do as I say. Fine."

He put the phone down. His fingers played with his wedding ring, twisting it to the end of his finger, over the nail onto his thumb, then flicked it back onto his finger again. Kata was wrong. The little boy who had heard his mother sob late into the night before rising early to clean up the filth of his "betters" knew she was wrong. And after his mother's early death the boy who had hid terrified behind his grandmother's skirts as his father lurched at him in yet another rage remembered everything. How she would calm his father down until he fell weeping into sleep. Then she would tend the little boy's hurts and he would sit in the firelight listening to her stories. She would read the leaves, or deal his cards.

"You are going to be a powerful man, one day, my little Gio. It is all here. But you must beware of a woman. She will destroy you. And listen to your dreams, my little one. Listen to your dreams."

Now, in the cold light of day, Mac had forgotten nothing. His dream meant something. What he couldn't yet tell. But he was going to the top. His grandmother had seen it in the cards. And nothing, or no-one was going to stop him.

Plans

❧ ❧

Mac looked at his watch. 10.40. They would be here soon. He made sure the door from the hall was open so that they could see the gym from the front door. And Carla had a key.

He climbed painfully onto the exercise bike. He began to peddle. The effort was excruciating. He pushed. Harder. He was breaking into a sweat. He threw back his head and took a deep breath. With relief he heard the sound of car tyres against the gravel. He heard voices, Carla's key turning softly in the door.

"Mr Maconi said to let ourselves in. Signora Maconi is at the hospital with her mother."

The door opened. Mac peddled furiously.

Giorgio stood in the hallway.

"Much recovered I see."

"Ah. Giorgio. Yes. What is the time? Are you early?"

He took the towel from the handlebars and slung it around his neck.

"Will you wait in the lounge please? I shall be there in a moment."

He watched them turn down the corridor and into the lounge. He caught a worried look from Carla, but nothing in his face betrayed the agony in his legs. He got down from the bike and wiped the sweat from his face. Then he took a glass of water from the table and walked smiling into the lounge.

"Now what can I do for you?"

"I'm glad to see you up and about. From what the doctors had said I hadn't expected to see you back in the gym for a while."

"I told you I was much better. I can't let myself turn to flab can I? If a man doesn't have control over himself how can he have control over his department?"

Mac sat down, swinging his feet onto the other end of the sofa.

"Kata said you were still in a bad way."

"Kata worries. She's a woman. Ask Carla. Do you worry too Carla?"

The question was condescending. Carla knew it, but answered none the less.

"Yeah, sure I worry. But not about Mr Maconi. He's like an elephant. It would take more than a juggernaut to bring him down."

Mac looked at her. Yes, she was good. Cool as a cucumber. He wondered if she had guessed how much pain he was in. If she had her face showed no sign of it. Unless, of course, she really didn't care how he was. But somehow he doubted that. Sweet little Carla. His eyes wandered across her body. He took in the full breasts, the rounded hips. She was not what he would describe as beautiful, but there was fire there. Yes, little Carla could be quite a tiger when roused. And she was unquestioningly loyal. Quite an asset. He would take her with him when he moved up. He caught her eye and flashed her a bemused smile. She knew where her bread was buttered.

"Now those contracts."

Mac studied the documents and made comments. He knew the real reason that Giorgio was there. It had nothing to do with the contracts. They could have been done by anyone.

43

Carla, certainly. No, Giorgio Paccini was there to make sure the "ice man" could still cut it. And Mac was going to give him a show. The pain was rising in him now. It felt as though every pore in his legs was bleeding. He showed no emotion.

Finally Giorgio picked up his briefcase and announced it was time to go.

"They are making the decision tomorrow, Mac."

"Decision?"

"About the new head of European Acquisitions. I shall put in a good word for you."

"Thank you."

They turned and went.

Carla put the briefcase into the boot of the car then returned to the house closing the door so that Giorgio couldn't see.

"That was quite some act."

"Act?" Mac's voice was shaking ever so slightly.

"Painkillers?"

"On the shelf. Two."

Carla silently handed him the tablets and watched as he gulped the water down.

"I wonder if I will be there?" she asked him.

"When?"

"The day the ice man melts."

"Not a chance."

Then she turned on her heels and left.

Mac hauled himself up onto the sofa and breathed deeply. By the time his wife returned he was fast asleep.

A Little Deception

≈ ⋘

Rhian walked over to Elen and sat down. She looked even more smug than usual.

"Now say 'thank you' and tell me I'm the best friend you ever had"

Elen looked at her quizzically. This sounded like trouble.

"Ok, Cheshire cat, what have you done."

"Set you up with a date with your dream boy, that's all!"

Elen was aghast.

"You have done what? With whom? Rhi, you have gone too far this time. You had better go find whoever it is and tell him you have got it wrong. And boy, have you got it wrong…"

Rhian interrupted.

"Relax, will you. I ran into Splodge and Bag Boy and invited them to Mammy's evening do on Saturday. That's all. No major drama."

'Ran into' wasn't exactly telling the truth. She had feigned a stomach upset to get out of John Jenkins lecture and had wandered round the college carrying her brother's leather wallet wandering into as many rooms as she dared enquiring after it's "owner". Once she had found the room the boys were in she had waited half way up the stairs until people started to come out of the rooms. Then she pushed her way up the stairs 'accidentally' bumping into Splodge. But she wasn't going to tell Elen any of that. Her mission had been successful and there was no need for details.

John Jenkins walked into the refectory obviously looking for Rhian. Elen nudged her friend. Rhian turned visibly pale and shoved her beef burger into her bag. She clutched her stomach and twisted her face as if in great pain. The lecturer walked over to them.

"Are you alright Rhian? You didn't come back into the lecture."

Rhian looked at him pathetically.

"Oh thank you for your concern Mr Jenkins. I was SO ill. It must be a bug. Elen's been feeling queasy as well, haven't you?"

Elen looked alarmed. Lying was not her strong point. Before she could answer Mr Jenkins stepped back and looked at them both.

"I really don't think it's a good idea to come into college when you are ill and spread your germs around. Particularly when you have a large block of teaching practice starting next week. I think you should both go home and not come back until you are quite well."

The girls nodded. Rhian picked up her bag, carefully, so that the beef burger didn't fall out and spoil the show.

"It's probably just a twenty four hour bug. I'm sure we will both be right as rain by tomorrow."

John Jenkins turned on his heels and left. Elen was speechless. Rhian grabbed her arm and limped weakly out of the college. As they turned the corner by the sports hall Elen found her voice.

"What the blue blazes are you playing at?"

Rhian giggled.

"Good wasn't I? They should put me up for an award."

"Award for what? Looniest girl on the planet? What was all that about?"

Rhian looked genuinely hurt.

"Look here Elen. I'm just trying to do you a favour."

"I don't need any favours thank you."

"Ok, so tell me you AREN'T interested in Rhys Harris then. Tell me you DON'T want to go into Cardiff and find a killer outfit that will have his tongue on the floor. You are doing just fine on your little lonesome. Elen Lloyd if it's left to you, you will still be an old maid when you're forty. Someone had to give you a push."

"Ok. Ok. Thank you. I'm just not sure I want to be pushed."

Rhian got into the car and retrieved the beef burger.

"Yuk, the mustard has gone all over my file."

"Serves you right for lying."

"I wasn't lying. I am sick."

Elen looked at her disbelievingly.

"I am. Sick with lust for the lovely Simon Lodge. Come on, where shall we go first? I really do think you should get a wonderbra to make the most of your assets. Guys can never resist the possibility of a bosom. "

Elen shook her head.

"You take the biscuit, you really do."

Rhian grinned as she finished off the last of the beef burger.

"Nah – I'm on a diet."

Moving Up

୬ ๙

"Well, Mac, how do you like your new office?"

Giorgio smiled as Mac ran his hand along the walnut contours of his new desk. He savoured the moment. The boy from the back streets was on his way. He looked out of the window across the square with its elegant fountains. He breathed in deeply.

"It's good, Giorgio. It's good. I feel as though I belong here."

His colleague eyed him with interest. Mac Maconi was a dangerous customer. He had clawed his way up from the bottom of the pile with stealth as well as ability. His bosses had already realised it would never be safe to turn their back whilst Mac was around. But, of course, they had to keep his skills within the organisation. Which was why they had decided on their next move.

"Don't get too comfortable"

"Why? Do you think I won't stay the course?"

Mac's tone was friendly but there was a hard edge to it that Giorgio distrusted.

"You are off to the UK. There's a little project there that the top corridor want you to take a look at. Size it up. Acquire it. At a price that suits us, of course."

Giorgio handed Mac a file. Mac glanced through the first couple of pages.

"What you mean is, you want me to go in there, convince them we are doing them a favour by buying them out and then cream off the profits."

He voice was flat. No trace of emotion. This was his job, and he knew exactly how to do it. Giorgio knew this too.

"You leave on Thursday."

Mac nodded. He escorted his colleague out of his office and into the smaller space where his new "team" were already busy.

"Where's your lovely second in command today?"

Mac gave a half smile.

"Carla? I gave her some time off today. Her boyfriend is coming home tonight and she wanted to arrange something special for him."

"Mac Maconi getting sentimental in his dotage?"

Giorgio looked for a clue in Mac's face. There was none.

"Carla has worked very hard keeping everything going while I was off. It pays to keep her sweet."

Mac closed the door. Yes, it did pay to keep Carla sweet. She was his eyes and ears. No-one thought to keep secrets from the unassuming brunette. Mac knew he would have been passed over for this promotion without Carla's "information". If truth were told it was Carla, not Mac, who had done the essential work on the contracts Giorgio had brought over after his accident. She was one person he intended to keep very sweet indeed.

Then he turned his attention to the file. A sizable electronics company in South Wales, making a reasonable profit. But also making components they wanted at a much much cheaper price. This was going to be a challenge. Mac's eyes flashed. This was going to be fun.

The Butterfly

꙳   ꙳

Elen looked at her reflection in the mirror as she dried her hair. She could see the similarities with her memories of her mother when she was a child. The same cupids bow mouth, the same dark hair, although she had her father's deep blue eyes. She wondered how her mother would have felt to see her all dressed up and ready to go out tonight. Was she watching from whatever place souls go to? Without thinking her hand went to the picture frame on her bedside table. Its pale blue paint was chipped in places but she would never part with it. All along the edges it was covered in butterflies. She remembered her mother's words when she gave it to her, on her first day at junior school.

"Do you see the butterflies, Elen?"

She had nodded, tracing their exquisite outline with her small finger.

"We are all like butterflies. We all have it within us to be beautiful, enchanting. But we all get butterflies when we have to do something new. We have to remember that the butterfly was once an ugly caterpillar. Just as the caterpillar thought its world was ending, it realised it had turned into a butterfly. Have courage. Everything will be fine."

And it was. She had lived a happy, loving childhood. Nothing troubled her. No childhood drama was too big to be unravelled into little manageable pieces by gentle words. Until her mother became ill. Hushed tones as she walked in the door. She looked so tired. No one would tell Elen what was going on. Then her mother took her on her knee and explained gently that she had a door that she had to go through. She did not know what lay on the other side but this was what was prepared for her. Elen was not to be afraid. She would always be with her, even when she couldn't see or touch her. But where was she now?

It had been nine years since her death. Already Elen found her image was beginning to fade and she had to fight to recall her smile, the sound of her voice. But she had made Elen in her own image and Elen knew it. She could no more escape becoming like her mother than she could escape breathing.

She struggled to think back. They had one last Christmas together before she died, peacefully, at the hospice. They had done everything as she wished. The flowers, the hymns at the funeral – all chosen by her mother before her death. Every detail had been carefully written down and adhered to. Her mother said that knowing death was around the corner was a privilege. It allowed you to make your peace with everyone and to arrange everything to cause the least pain to those you love. How much better, she had said, than to be taken suddenly, with no time to say goodbye.

For those left behind, it was no easier. After the initial relief at seeing her at last released from pain, came an unbearable longing to have her back. Sometimes she would wake, even now, and forget that she had gone. Morning bringing the same dull ache. Her mother had promised her it would get easier. And so it did. But tonight, as she stood ready to go out to meet the first boy she felt she might really fall for, she missed her mother so very much.

The beep of her phone pulled her back into the here and

now. Rhian. Could she borrow Elen's hair straighteners? Apparently her hair had completely frizzed in the afternoon drizzle standing outside the registry office and she simply could NOT seduce the lovely Simon looking like an extra from the bride of Frankenstein. Elen wondered if she was referring to her mother's nuptials, but decided against commenting. She texted back that she was on her way with hair serum and straighteners. Then she grabbed her bag, said a hurried goodbye to her father and headed for the door.

"What time will you be in, love?"

Her dad sounded tired.

"Not too late, dad. They chuck us out at twelve. So I should be in just after that. If I go the distance!"

He smiled.

"At least you don't have to worry about getting Rhian home tonight. She really is a girl and a half that one!"

"She certainly is. And I have to go and sort her hair out. She's on the pull tonight."

Her father grimaced.

"Who's the innocent she has set her sights on this time?"

"A boy from college. Although I don't think he knows it yet."

She shook her head.

"Like a lamb to the slaughter. Anyway. See you in the morning. Don't wait up"

She kissed her father on the forehead and closed the door behind her. She had been careful not to mention anything about Rhys to him. Why, she mused? She wasn't sure that anything was going to happen between them. She liked him, and there were definitely sparks, but he didn't seem to want to do anything about them. She took a deep breath.

"Ok. Let's see what tonight brings."

Exile

❧   ❧

Giorgio was going over last minute details with Mac before he departed for the UK. Mac already knew the company's details off by heart. He had memorised the face and details of each of the board members. By this time next week he would have added to that, their weaknesses – each one of which he would exploit. That was the name of the game.

Carla came in with the latest figures.

"That's a pretty little gem around your neck, Carla. I don't think I've seen that before."

Giorgio was always attentive. Carla fingered the pink diamond pendant on its delicate platinum chain. It was, indeed, very pretty.

"Thank you. It was a gift from my boyfriend."

"Was it now? He must be serious about you Carla. Are you serious about him?"

Carla looked flustered. Mac came to her rescue.

"I hate to break your heart Giorgio, but I think our little Carla is in love. She has been purring like a kitten ever since her rendezvous with her mystery man on Tuesday, haven't you Carla. He's a lucky man, wouldn't you say?"

Carla blushed furiously and backed out of the room. She sat at her desk and put her hands to her face to cool it. Was she in love? Was it love that made her fantasize and long for every kiss? Was it love that made her forget all reason, blind to the faults of the object of her affection, caring only that he wanted her? Love that makes giddy teenagers of us all, cocooning us in it's warm rose mist, clouding everything. Its spell only to be broken by the shattering of an uncared for heart as it falls to the floor. Carla knew she should be careful. But all she could think of was their last night of passion together. She recalled the warmth of his hands as they fastened the trinket around her neck and the soft words.

"I want them to know you are mine, Carla."

"Who?"

Their voices were barely a whisper.

"All the men in the world. Every man that looks at you and wants you, the way I want you now."

"And are you mine?"

"You belong to me. Every kiss. Every sigh. Every inch of you belongs to me."

Then he kissed her with such exquisite tenderness that she forgot that he had side stepped the question.

Half an hour later Mac was breezing out of the office on his way to the airport. Carla was to join him there next week as there were still a few loose ends to tie up at that end. Mac whistled as he walked towards the terminal. They had given him quite a tough job as his first assignment, but nothing that he thought he couldn't handle. Things were shaping up just the way he wanted.

A couple of hours later the plane touched down at Cardiff Airport. Not exactly the metropolis he was expecting. The drizzle soaked his coat as he walked the short distance from the plane to the terminal. The wind was up and blowing the fine droplets of water into his face. He had forgotten how cold Britain was. A cold and inhospitable country he had always thought. He looked around him as he hailed a taxi. So this was Wales.

The Best Laid Plans of Valley Girls

☙ ❧

The music blasted out from the disco. As yet no-one was dancing, but it was early in the night and people were still chatting and drinking. Elen and Rhian had positioned themselves opposite the door in order to have the best possible view of the arriving guests. Rhian was fiddling with the hem of her dress. It was, as Elen had pointed out when she bought it, more than a little on the short side. Rhian's generous figure pulled the fabric up further than was perhaps intended (although she insisted she actually was a size 14 not a 16) and it was barely decent when she walked. As it was, sitting was decidedly precarious! The dress was red satin, cut indecently low at both front and back. Rhian had been aiming for Liv Tyler, but the look was definitely more Lili Savage. Every time she moved her arms her bosom threatened to escape. Elen suggested it might look better if she put her jacket over it.

"After all, you don't want to put all your items at the front of the shop now do you?" she ventured.

Rhian was undeterred.

"If you've got it, flaunt it" was her curt reply. And no-one could accuse Rhian of *not* flaunting it!

Elen had agonised over what to wear. Where as Rhian always went for minimum fabric stretched as tightly as humanly possible, Elen preferred not to show too much flesh. It wasn't that she didn't have a good figure, she was slim but with curves in the right places. It was more a question of having the confidence to carry it off. She had chosen a pale pink chiffon dress with a handkerchief hemline which skimmed her calf. It had tiny lines of glitter which caught the light. As she had looked in the mirror the figure looking back at her surprised her. She had grown up. She actually looked elegant. When did that happen? And how? Was the caterpillar becoming a butterfly at last?

It was 9.30pm and there was still no sign of the boys. The buffet had been unveiled and the DJ was going into overdrive. Next track up was "Dancing Queen". So, of course, there was no option but to leave their door view vigil and take to the floor. Half way through the first chorus they were joined by Splodge and Rhys. Rhian beamed and turned her body towards him to give him a better view of her undulating charms. Rhys looked shyly at Elen and turned towards her. He was dressed in smart jeans and a well fitting light blue T shirt. Very well fitting. Elen took in the shape of his upper body. He was bigger than she had imagined. His arms were well defined and the muscles beneath his T shirt looked firm. She watched the way his body moved. He really was a surprisingly good dancer. He had rhythm. He didn't look like a frog in a blender. All the men she had ever met that could dance were either gay or very camp but there was nothing effeminate about Rhys's movements. He was so, well, manly. Curls of dark chest hair were visible over the neck of his T shirt. She glanced up to find him looking intently at her. She wondered if he had guessed her thoughts and reddened. She was grateful when the track ended and she had an excuse to sit down.

Rhys followed her. As she sat down he asked her what she would like to drink and then obediently went off to the bar to get her orange juice. He was ages at the bar. It is always the same at weddings. The management always underestimates the number of bar staff required and everyone ends up queuing for half an hour. Then people get the hang of it and order 2 rounds at once. Which means it takes twice as long to get served…

Elen watched Rhian in action on the dance floor. Shrinking violet she was not. She was strutting her stuff and it clearly had Splodge mesmerised. He eyes never moved above breast level for at least the next three tracks. Was she right, Elen wondered? Was that really the way to get a guy? Her upbringing had told her that all you would get that way were boys who were interested in your body but nothing more. Was that right? Was that all that Rhian was looking for? Elen wasn't looking to settle down – the thought terrified her, but she wanted a relationship that *meant* something.

She looked back at Rhys who was now making his way back with the drinks. He sat down. They both sat in silence for a few minutes. It would have been hard enough to make conversation under normal circumstances but in the din of the disco they had to shout to make themselves heard. The other by product of the noise was that they had to get very close in order to hear what the other person was saying. Rhys had begun his teaching practice in a school not far from where Elen lived. Although he had started out wanting to teach secondary pupils he had had to do two weeks in a primary school and much to his surprise he really loved it.

"You get so much back from the kids" he enthused.

"They really want to know stuff. It's like *everything* fascinates them. They really really want to learn. Do you know what I mean?"

"Yes, I know exactly what you mean. I've been in my school now for nearly a term. When I get there in the morning there is always a crowd of kids waiting to say hello, waiting to give me their news or show me their new toy or tell me what they watched on television last night. Every day is an adventure to them."

Elen's love of her job shone in her eyes. They looked at each other and smiled. Maybe there was common ground here. It seemed as if they both saw the world from the same perspective. They talked all night. Rhys learnt that Elen adored the children she taught. There was something special about every one of them. You could feel the affection flowing through her.

"They give you so much, children. Their trust, their time, their love."

Rhys could see that love reflected from her and told her so.

"That's the thing about love." He added softly.

"You don't absorb it. It just shines through you and reflects onto everyone else. People who love and give love glow."

"Do I glow?" she asked.

"You glow. Like sunlight through a crystal."

Then they both got embarrassed and looked at their feet. Elen broke the silence.

"The thing is… I don't want to sound forward or anything… but I really like to get to know people before I… err…"

Rhys looked relieved.

"Me too. Splodge is the one night stand merchant – although I don't really think he has pulled anywhere near as often as he claims he has.."

They both laughed and looked out to the dance floor where Rhian and Splodge were now oblivious to everyone else, wrapped in each other's arms and getting to know each other in an entirely different way.

Rhys looked at Elen nervously.

"What are you doing next weekend?"

"Meal with my father on Sunday – it's my birthday."

"Oh. Happy birthday. For Sunday."

"I've nothing planned on Saturday though."

Rhys brightened.

"Would you like to go somewhere? We could have a day out. For your birthday. What sort of places do you like to go?"

Elen smiled back happily.

"I don't mind. I'm doing a project for the kids at the moment. If we could go somewhere I could get some info on that it would be really useful."

"Ok. I'll get my books out and sort out the best place to go. As friends, of course."

"Of course."

Castles in the Air

❧　❧

From Mac's hotel room he could see a very large square castle. Nothing like the elegant monuments in Rome but impressive none the less. It was square and very large. Roman, he was told, restored by someone called Burgess. He ate his breakfast (what is it with the British that they want to eat so much animal for breakfast?) and then went down to reception. He arranged a hire car for the next day. He wanted to get the feel of the place before he headed off to the factory tomorrow for his initial meeting. The receptionist was very helpful. She had guide brochures and a video on what to see in the area. Mac took them back to his room. He began flicking through them then lost interest and wandered down into the city.

The driving rain of last night had given way to hazy sunshine. It promised to be a glorious day. Cardiff in the autumn sunlight was quite pleasant. Not too busy and the roads were wide. It looked British, but not English somehow. The road signs were in two languages. As he stood at reception waiting for the taxi a couple passed him speaking what he presumed to be Welsh. Something about this old tongue sent a shiver through him.

Cardiff was not what he had expected. It was small for a city, its wide streets lined with a curious tapestry of Victorian and modern buildings. He walked alongside the castle and then turned into the main shopping area. There were the usual city shops, chain stores and designer brands, but there were also stalls selling locally made crafts, glassware, jewellery, pottery and woodwork. Other shops sold Welsh goods, flags, clothes and a whole host of other items that seemed totally alien to him.

He ate his lunch in a modern well lit café on the newly refurbished waterfront. He looked out onto the bay and the millennium centre. All around him was that strange accent, obviously British but with a musical lilt and a metre that seemed to have a poetry of its own. Here and there he caught snatches of Welsh. A fast paced but ancient sounding tongue. Each sentence sounded like an incantation. He had no idea the language was so widely spoken. Even children on the street were using it with each other. Mac found himself drawn into their conversation, straining to make out something he could understand. He had a good grounding of languages. His father was Spanish, his grandmother pure bred Romany, so there had been a mixture of languages in his household from his childhood. Being multi-lingual seemed a natural state. Everyone learnt English and French at school. In a modern Europe it made commercial sense to be able to negotiate in the customer's native tongue. Mac's flair with languages had given him an extra edge.

His mind clicked forward to tomorrow's business tasks. He wondered if his inability to speak Welsh might prove a hindrance. He had been told that it wasn't widely spoken in the South, but the books he had studied on the plane showed that the percentage was higher than he had been led to believe — particularly amongst the more affluent classes. Would that include the company directors he wondered? To be on the safe side he walked back to one of the shops he had seen selling Welsh books and music. He asked for advice on which book to buy and settled on a cd rom which would give him the basics in the language. He headed back to his hotel to try it out on his laptop. He made himself a cup of coffee and switched on the TV to catch up with the international news. He noted the changes in the markets that might affect him and the way the business wind was currently blowing. He left it running as he studied his files, glancing up now and again if something caught his ear. He looked at the clock. It would soon be time to eat. He was just about to switch off the TV and get ready for dinner when his eye landed on the tourist dvd he had borrowed from reception that morning.

He had felt strangely restless today. He couldn't seem to focus on the task in hand. He decided to watch the video. It might give him a bit more local knowledge and certainly it would be a diversion. Mac knew he was talking himself into this – it was a "pencil case tidying exercise" which whilst it could be justified on one level was ultimately getting in the way of what he really should be doing. He put the disk in the machine and hit the play button. His attention wandered. He saw the famed rolling hills, the sandy beaches, the rivers and then something stopped him in his tracks. He had been half watching a piece about the castle opposite his hotel when another castle was shown. Mac stood rooted to the spot. It was the castle from his dream.

As the video progressed he felt a cold breath move through his body. He remembered each room, the decorations on the walls, the butterflies around the archway. Suddenly Mac found he could focus again. Very clearly. It was a sign, he was sure of it. Something had made sure he had come to Wales. His future depended on it. Something very special was about to happen. He wound the programme back to find the name of the place. Castell Coch. It was in Cardiff, only a few miles from where he was staying now. He looked at his watch. It was too late to head out today and he would be far too busy tomorrow. He had to just see it though, to be sure.

He walked down to reception to find out how to get to the castle. The receptionist knew all about it and had lots of leaflets. Mac watched her as she searched. Long red hair tied in a ponytail. He wondered what she would look like with her hair loose. As she leant forward he took the opportunity to appraise her cleavage. Her eyes met his and she blushed. Mac did not. She found some brochures on the castle for him. Yes. This was the one all right. He checked the opening hours. There was no way he would be there before it closed. Mac felt that if he could just see it from the outside. Then he would know.

There was a tour bus. Mac didn't fancy that. So the receptionist dutifully arranged a taxi. The taxi duly arrived. The driver was pleasant enough and pointed out landmarks on the way. The shops and arcades, the museum, the old city hall. The driver drawled on as they were stuck in yet another stream of traffic. It was rush hour and the roads out of the city were gridlocked. Every mile seemed to take an age. The sun was setting casting an apricot glow over the mountains. They left the city centre and headed out towards the valleys. Then suddenly, Mac could see it.

It was not the way British castles were supposed to look, with its three round red towers and their green conical roofs. It almost grew out of the mountain. It looked somehow totally out of place and yet in perfect keeping with its surroundings. The departing day draped the building in an ethereal light, almost as though it couldn't possibly be real. Floodlights came on, casting eerie shadows which seemed to bounce off the round walls at strange angles. It could almost be a gateway to another world, or another time.

Mac shivered. Then he told the driver to head back to the hotel. He had work to do.

The Suitor

❧ ❦

It was a bright winter's morning. The overnight frost had bejewelled the spiders webs and left the hedges sparkling. Soon they would melt back into ordinariness under the warmth of the sun which was already making its way into the clear blue sky. Rhys found himself wondering if they minded being so suddenly robbed of the finery they had so recently acquired. He whistled to himself as he walked to the car. Nothing could dent his spirits today. In his hand was the carefully chosen book for Elen's birthday. He had been relieved when she had made it clear she was someone who liked to take things slowly. Seeing the speed at which Rhian and Splodge had moved had unnerved him. Yes, he found Elen attractive, very attractive in fact, but there was something more there. She seemed to have an inner light and when she was talking about things she loved that light grew brighter. It made his heart soar to observe it. He knew he was on dangerous ground here. An inner sense told him that he was in serious danger of falling in love with this girl. And that was a very scary proposition.

He turned the car out of his native valley and up towards the Rhigos mountain. Even on a clear day like today the top of the mountain was shrouded in mist. He passed fields of bored looking sheep who studied him silently as the car passed. He could almost hear the conversation after he had gone.

"Told you it would be a silver one"

"No you didn't. You said red."

But of course all the passer by would have heard was "Baa".

The road began to climb steeply now and bend alarmingly. Rhys loved this mountain. It had a totally untameable quality. It seemed to him that a person could lose all sense of time and place on this wild rugged hillside. No wonder the ancients had seen such places as somewhere to communicate with the gods. Here earth and sky merged. Even in the twenty first century it felt other–worldly. The rust coloured scrub already had hints of deep green showing from below. In the depths of winter spring was already making plans for her return. That was the way of the world. As it was for the ancients, so it was still now. Nothing changed on the face of the old mountain. It knew its place and it knew yours.

Rhys rounded the top of the mountain and held his breath. As the car turned to make the descent into the valley he was well rewarded, as he knew he would be. The majesty that was the Rhondda opened up before him. The craggy landscape bathed with a myriad of colours under the gentle winter sunlight, each ray softly waking a new stretch of grassland, or heather or tall deep green pines. At each bend another wonder came into view. His own birthplace might have once have been known as "The Queen of the Valleys" but surely, the Rhondda was the most beautiful.

The view was again masked by trees as Rhys turned the last bend and drove into Treherbert. Elen lived in a little village between Treherbert and the next town, Treorci. The latter, he had been told, was named after the communist "Gorky", although he wasn't sure if that was just a myth. He made a mental note to find out. After all, if he was going to be going out with a girl from that area it was only good manners to find out all he could about where she came from.

The thought brought him right back to reality. Somehow or other he had got to get around to asking her out properly today. It was his big chance. He had arranged things to perfection. He had picked the most romantic place he could think of, brought along a picnic and had her present wrapped up in pink paper tied with a bow. He knew she liked pink. He remembered the tag on her bag and the number of times her had seen her wearing the colour. Every detail was stamped indelibly on his memory.

The sun was smiling on them, so it seemed that even nature was giving him a nudge, saying "Go on Rhys, go for it!"

He checked his directions and turned into the next street of heavy stone terraced houses. He counted along them and stopped outside the one with the red door. He took a deep breath.

"Here we go…"

The Negotiator

᷿ ᷿

Mac smiled to himself. The initial meeting had gone well, very well. He had already managed to convince the board of directors that their firm was in dire straits and that if S-Systems didn't come along to "bail them out" they could lose everything. He hadn't bent the truth exactly, but let's just say that he had given the view from his perspective. Which was what he was supposed to do. He had certainly given them a lot to think about. His figures were absolutely spot on, he had made sure of that. He had no doubt that by Monday they would be clamouring for further talks.

His hand went instinctively to his pocket as it always did when he was apprehensive. His fingers touched the cold metal of the talisman his grandmother had given him. It was an old coin – Roman she had told him, although it was now so worn that it could have been anything – fastened into a frame to make a key ring. Part of him wanted to dismiss such mumbo jumbo. It didn't fit in with his hi-tech hard nosed world. But he could never quite let go of such ideas. He remembered the house by the lake, where worried women would come to see Bibi, desperate for comfort. She would make the tea, listen to their worries as they drank, then turn the cup and read what she saw. Sometimes it would be good news, sometimes bad, but always they left the house a little lighter. No one paid any attention to the small boy sitting on the stairs. If his grandmother noticed him she would simply nod and smile. It was the order of things. Life was simple, she used to tell him. Only consequences are harder to live with in their moment.

Mac sighed. He ordered half a bottle of red wine with his dinner at the hotel restaurant. He wondered if he would drink it. He thought not. He was tired. He still wasn't a hundred percent after the accident, a fact that he betrayed to no-one, not even Carla or Kata. But it had taken its toll. Bibi knew, of course. But she had not tried to persuade him against taking this trip. An early night, tonight, he decided. Then tomorrow, he would go and take a look at that castle. In the light of day he had been less sure that it was the castle from his dream. After all, he was a grown man. It was he who was in charge of his destiny, not some supernatural force. He took a sip of wine and sat back in his seat.

"Listen to your dreams" his grandmother had said.

Never the less, he reasoned, it wouldn't hurt to take a look.

The Date

☙　❧

Elen was looking out of the window when Rhys pulled up outside the house. She opened the door with a smile and called to him.

"Be with you now, in a minute."

Rhys nodded and got back into the car and turned on the radio. He was away with the fairies when she knocked the passenger door window a few minutes later. He jumped and she laughed out loud. He opened the door and put her coat on the back seat.

"Sorry I didn't ask you in, but if Dad had started his 20 questions routine we wouldn't have been there by tea time."

Rhys smiled back at her. His tongue and brain had been disconnected again. He started up the car, reaching fruitlessly in his mind for something to say.

"Where *are* we going exactly?" she asked.

"Surprise." He answered.

"Wait and see"

Elen wasn't sure if she liked surprises, but it did seem a romantic thing to do. She hadn't expected him to take charge. She smiled to herself. There was more to Rhys Harris than met the eye. The car headed off down the valley. Elen wondered if they were going to the coast, although perhaps it would be a bit cold for a stroll along the beach. They turned onto the dual carriageway. They both began to relax a bit more now.

"How is your stint in the comprehensive school going?"

Elen had remembered that Rhys had started a new block of teaching practice that week.

"Less like teaching – more like lion taming!"

"I wonder what it is that happens to children over the six week school holiday that turns them into monsters?"

Rhys laughed – with his whole face. His eyes sparkled. Elen smiled back. He certainly had something special. Would it be enough though? She watched the relaxed way he held the steering wheel as he drove. His hands were broad, like the rest of him – strong. His forearms were tanned. She really did like him. Rhys was oblivious and carried on the conversation unaware of her interest or admiration.

"To be fair, I think it's the system. At junior school they develop a trusting relationship with their teacher and they aren't expected to act like grown ups. They get to comprehensive school and everything has changed.

"I see what you mean. They now have different teachers for every subject"

"Yeah, and they may not be in the same class with all their friends, so that's stressful and the teachers expect them to behave differently."

"And so they do – but not the way the teachers want them to"

"That's part of it. Add to that the hormones that are pumping their way through their bodies and their bad eating habits – do you know most of them go out in the morning without eating breakfast. By break time they are too hungry to concentrate."

Elen looked at him with new eyes. He really cared about the pupils he taught.

"You are going to make a good teacher Rhys Harris."

70

Rhys blushed but couldn't help break out into a broad grin at the compliment.

"Here we are."

They took a left turn off the road and into a long wooded lane, parking in a car park at the top of the hill.

"Perfect."

Searching for a Princess

❧   ❧

Mac strolled down to reception to meet his taxi. He looked at his watch. He was impatient now. If there was one thing that taxi firms across the entire world have in common it was their propensity to tardiness. Mac was never late. Eventually the black mondeo arrived with its driver muttering apologies and complaining about the unexpected traffic. Mac nodded and got into to the back and confirmed his destination with the driver. Castell Coch. The driver drove around the walls of Cardiff Castle and up towards the northern edge of the city. The road widened and their speed picked up. They turned off the dual carriageway and into a small village. The traffic moved so slowly. He felt that it would have been quicker to get out and walk. This was what some of the American tourists were doing. You could spot them a mile off with their brightly mismatched clothes and even louder accents. The taxi turned a sharp right and began to climb. The narrow road turned and twisted its way upwards. Mac thought that they would never get there. And then, suddenly, there he was.

The entrance wound up a long steep hill. The driver dropped him off half way up at the car park. Mac took his card and told him that he would ring when he was ready to leave. The pathway was dappled by sunlight. Mac felt as if he was walking back in time itself. There was hardly anyone around.

This could have been any century. King Arthur and all of his knights could have ridden past and he wouldn't have batted an eyelid. The castle seemed to have an enchantment all of its own and he was under its spell. And what of the girl of his dreams? Would she be there, like the fabled sleeping beauty, or was he just imagining it all.

Mac went over the drawbridge and paid his fee at the kiosk. Now he realised just how hazy his dream was. He had no real idea of where he had to go. Up some steps. He found himself in the chapel. No, that wasn't right. Up more steps. Into Lady Margaret's room. No that wasn't the one either. He crossed the courtyard and into another tower. He found an exhibition. No. This wasn't right either. He began to panic. Was it all nothing more than a dream?

Back into the courtyard. Two young lads raced past him with flaming red hair. Yes. He remembered that. Where had they come from?

The Date Continues

– –

Rhys finished the last of their picnic and put the cups back into the wicker hamper. Things were going well. They seemed to be getting on very well indeed. Elen watched him closely. She couldn't decide what was going on here. He was friendly, affectionate in fact, but she wasn't at all certain that he wanted anything more than friendship. They had spent all morning together and he hadn't made the slightest notion of a move.

Just then a child's voice shouted out

"Miss Lloyd!"

A small bespectacled six year old was waving frantically and running towards them.

"One of your pupils?"

Rhys was amused.

"Yes, Hefin Lewis. I've been teaching him all term. He's lovely, but very enthusiastic."

This was borne out when the boy came crashing into her seconds later.

"Miss Lloyd – have you seen the dungeon? It's so cool here!"

His speech was like machine gun fire, no pause for punctuation, just an endless stream of energy. His grandfather walked over to them.

"You must be the famed Miss Lloyd. We have heard a lot

about you. I don't know what you have been doing to Hefin but all of a sudden he actually *wants* to read. Hefin, put your teacher down, she isn't here on school business."

Hefin was undeterred.

"Granddad says I can't go up to see the bedrooms cos the stairs are too steep. Will you take me, Miss?"

The young boy's eyes were shining.

"You said there were monkeys on the walls, Miss. Please can we go and see the monkeys?"

Rhys laughed.

"I'll put these back in the car and meet you back in the courtyard in fifteen minutes. You had better go play teacher or you will break some one's heart there."

Elen blushed and nodded.

"See you in a bit then. Right, Mr Lewis. Let's go and find the monkeys."

Rhys waved to her as he passed through the gateway and crossed the drawbridge. She followed the excited child across the courtyard and into the banqueting hall. His grandfather followed and sat down on a chair.

"Thank you very much. Are you sure don't mind? I'll wait down here. My legs aren't up to that spiral staircase."

The elderly man was grateful and apologetic.

"No problem. It's nice to see someone so eager to learn."

"He's got too much energy for me. He hasn't stopped since we got here. At least he should sleep tonight!"

Elen tried to answer but she was aware that the boy was already halfway up the staircase, so she smiled, nodded and followed up quickly after him.

The Princess

ಾ ⤴

Mac walked into the Banqueting room. This was more like it. He remembered the figure of St Lucius over the fireplace. Already he could see the butterflies around the door into the drawing room. His heart leapt as he saw the figure of an old man resting in one of the chairs. Where was she? He heard footsteps on the stone stairs and a child's laughter. A young boy ran over to the old man. He stood up and smiled. The child ran back to someone.

"Grandad, you should have seen all the monkeys. And the bed with the magic balls on it. And everything looks so small from the windows. Can we go and see the windlass room with the big wheel that turns the drawbridge?"

The child hardly paused between sentences. Mac smiled at the enthusiasm of youth.

And there she was. Above her the sun was golden. Around her was a sky full of stars and birds. She stood, framed against animal figures. Lovely. Calm. But was she real? Mac held his breath. Then she walked through the door with its attendant butterflies, across the green carpet, stumbled where it met the tiled floor and fell — straight into his arms. The contents of her handbag spilled out onto the floor.

"Thank you" she gasped.

So, she was real. Mac's heart was pounding so hard that he

thought it would leap out of his chest. He breathed and took in the adrenalin rush. He adored that feeling of being on the brink of something new – almost losing control but never just quite.

Elen looked up and into the eyes of the most gorgeous man she had ever seen. He was perfect. Soft, olive coloured skin, even slim features, deep almost black eyes and a mouth that seemed to beg you to kiss it.

"You are welcome. Do you need to sit down?"

She smiled, a little uncertainly. She took in the details of his clothing. The elegant well cut suit, the detail on his shirt, the embroidery on the silk tie. Even his shoes were just right. Caramel leather echoing the stripe in the suit. His wavy black hair was slicked back but fell forwards over one eye. He looked as though he had just walked off a film set.

"Maybe. I just need a little air. I was going to sit outside for a while"

He stooped to pick up her belongings from the floor. He put them back into her bag. His hand lingered on hers as he handed them back to her. Mac's head was in a whirl. He hadn't felt this way since he was a teenager on a first date. Unsure of everything. What to say? What to do? He felt huge and clumsy beside her smallness.

"Let me come with you."

He held out his hand.

"Giovanni Maconi. Most people call me Mac"

"Elen Lloyd"

She looked up at him from long lashed eyes. Mac had to remember to breathe. His dream was replaying vividly now. And his grandmother's words echoed in his head.

"You know, you almost looked as if you were expecting me to fall."

She looked quizzical. Her face, the way her mouth turned up at the corners. It was all as he remembered it.

"I was. That is, I saw you start to fall."

"I see."

She was very quiet. Mac struggled to get his guard back in place. This whole thing was impossible. And yet there she was, living, breathing, beautiful. Every fibre in his body wanted her. Mac watched the sun glinting off her hair. The deep blue of her eyes. The gentle rise and fall of her breasts. He allowed himself to be lost in the moment – relishing it.

Then she smiled. The corners of her mouth curled up like a child's. There in that courtyard with its cobbled floor graced with curved red walls, time stood still. If ancient wizards had muttered incantations on that very spot then the magic was now leaching from every stone.

"Forgive me staring" he ventured.

"It is just that you are like a vision. With the sunlight in your hair in the magic of this place – you are the loveliest creature I have ever set eyes on"

Elen gazed back speechless at this alien creature. The sleek lines of his designer suit drew a sharp contrast to the smooth curves of the mock medieval castle. And yet somehow he looked as though he was meant to be there – like some knight in shining armour suddenly transported to modern times and given clothes appropriate to the occasion.

The spell was broken by the voice of a young man.

"There you are."

Rhys was walking briskly towards them across the cobbled courtyard. He looked slightly troubled to see Elen deep in conversation with Mac. Elen drew breath again. The world suddenly swung back to normal and she turned to face him.

"Rhys, this is Mac. He just caught me when I went flying in the banquet room. I guess castles and kitten heels really don't mix."

Rhys reached forward and shook Mac firmly by the hand.

The older man's grip was strong, stronger than Rhys's. They looked each other in the eye, neither blinking. Mac gave Rhys a warm smile.

"You are a lucky man. Your girlfriend is a very beautiful woman."

Rhys tried to reply but the words got stuck in his throat. Elen butted in quickly.

"Oh, Rhys isn't my boyfriend. We are just friends"

Mac took in the information but gave no visible reaction.

"We had better get going. They will be closing soon."

Rhys just wanted to get out of there and get Elen away from Mac as quickly as possible.

"Yes, I suppose we should. It was nice meeting you Mac. And thank you."

Mac took her hand and brought it to his cheek. "Thank you, Elen Lloyd. It has been my pleasure."

Then his lips brushed her skin with the softness of butterfly wings.

"Until we meet again."

Then she ran off across the courtyard and over the drawbridge.

Mac watched the elegance of her gait. Her hips swaying as she moved, long brown hair catching the sunlight. She turned to wave at him. The sunlight seemed to engulf her, like a mystical being. His fairy tale princess brought to life. Not a cold sleeping beauty, but a living breathing warm soft creature. Mac felt dizzy with excitement, weak with longing.

He waved back. Then he patted his pocket thoughtfully. His fingers clasped first Bibi's talisman and then they released to caress a small oblong object. He would meet Elen again. He was sure of it.

Misunderstandings

❧ ❧

Rhys sulked as they drove out of the car park. He had been all set to ask her to go out with him properly and now his plans had all gone awry. He had thought things were going perfectly. He had thought that she really liked him. Now his self confidence had been left on the cobbled floor of the courtyard under the shadow of that well dressed Italian.

"How is a man supposed to compete with that?" he thought.

His suit must have cost more than Rhys earned in a year in his part time job in the students union bar. Elen seemed to be really taken with him. She was very quiet as they drove back to the Rhondda. In reality Elen was having difficulty making sense of her feelings. She really thought that Rhys was going to make a move but he now he had gone decidedly cold on her. It wasn't her fault she had bumped into Mac. She hadn't flirted with him or even got his phone number, (although if truth was told she had seriously thought about it − but only for a few seconds). Now Rhys was behaving like a spoilt child. She didn't feel like massaging his ego and she was hurt by his apparent rejection.

"Men" she thought to herself.

"They are all the blooming same. They want more attention than five year olds. At least children tell you what is going on in their heads. Why do men have to go off in their metaphorical caves and sulk? I'm not a mind reader and I'm certainly not going to apologise for something I haven't done."

She stared out of the window. It was beginning to drizzle again, the weather a perfect mirror of the mood in the car. Rhys was fuming as they turned off the main road and headed for Treorci. Had she really fallen for all that smarm? The guy was slippier than a greased codfish. He stopped the car outside the stone terraced house with the brightly painted stone around the windows.

"Here we are then."

Elen was determined not to be churlish.

"Thank you for a lovely day Rhys. It was really very thoughtful of you."

Rhys blushed and began to wonder if he had mis-read things. Maybe she hadn't fallen for the smooth talking charmer after all. He reached into the back of the car.

"This is for you. Happy birthday for tomorrow."

She smiled. They looked into each other's eyes and Rhys gathered his courage ready to kiss her. In his head he could hear 10cc's "I'm not in love" playing softly.

"Elen – thank goodness you are home"

Elen's father was banging furiously on the car window. The needle scratched across Rhys's mental record as it ground abruptly to a halt. Elen wound the window down.

"What's the matter? Where's the fire?"

Elen too had been hoping for a magical moment and was more than annoyed at her father's intrusion.

"You've lost your phone. Some bloke rang the house to say he had found it. He's left his number."

"What?"

Elen hurriedly checked her bag. It was true. Her mobile phone was nowhere to be seen.

"It must have fallen out of my bag when I tripped up at the castle."

Rhys sat in silent bewilderment. He could not believe this was happening. Elen got out of the car and gathered her things together.

"Sorry Rhys. It has been a good day. I will have to go and sort this out. Can't believe I didn't realise I hadn't got my phone. I never even thought to check."

"No" thought Rhys, "you were too busy gazing into the eyes of Mr Smooth"

He did his best to smile.

"I'll ring you on Monday – or when I get the phone back. Thanks. It's been great. And thanks for the present."

She rushed off to the house with her father without even waving. Glumly Rhys started the engine and turned the car around. The rain was falling heavily now.

"Typical" he muttered.

He thumped the side of the car with his hand. It didn't respond. Rhys gave a sigh and headed for home.

Elen put her things down in the hall and tried to calm her flustered father down sufficiently to find out what had happened.

"Who rang? When? Where did he find it? What's the message?"

"This fella. He said he found your phone at Castell Coch. Here's his number."

He handed her a tatty piece of paper with a number scribbled on it.

"Dad. That's my number. I wonder how he got this one?"

"He said he looked in your contact list or something and found our number there. I don't understand these things. I don't know what's wrong with using a normal phone. We managed perfectly well when I was young..."

Elen nodded. Yes, she remembered putting the house number in her contact list as "ICE1" just in case there was ever an emergency and someone needed to contact her father. Rhian had said she was "off her head" at the time, but it looked as though it had paid off. She still wasn't sure how she could have lost her phone. She was sure that she had put all of her belongings back into her bag. There wasn't anything left on the floor. Maybe it had skidded sideways and gone out of view. She didn't like the idea of contacting a stranger – but whoever he was he had been kind enough to take the trouble to let her know he had the phone.

"Oh well, here goes nothing."

She rang the number. A familiar voice answered.

"Mac!"

Communication

❧ ❧

His voice was as soft and mellow. It inexplicably sent a tingling sensation through Elen's body.

"Your phone was on the bench where we sat down"

"Oh. I see"

She was flustered.

"Thank you for letting me know. I hadn't even realised that I had lost it."

"It just took a little detective work to find your number and there we are. Now, all we need to do is to make arrangements for me to get your shiny little silver phone back to its beautiful owner."

Elen hesitated, hoping that her hovering father hadn't taken in the fact that she was rose red.

"And how do you suggest we do that?"

"I think I have a simple but elegant solution."

"Yes?"

"Yes. You have dinner with me tonight, I can return your phone and I shall have the pleasure of the company of a lovely woman. What could be better? Do you think?"

Elen's head whirled. She felt the sudden need to sit down. Her stomach was doing all sorts of un-named dances. Before she could think clearly she heard herself saying

"Ok. Where shall I meet you?"

"There is a sweet little Italian restaurant in the side street near the theatre. I discovered it yesterday. Do you know where I mean?"

She knew.

"Yes, round the corner from the bank. I know it. I have been there before. The food is lovely."

"Ah, so you like Italian food. That is good. Shall we say eight o'clock? I shall wait outside for you. Or would you prefer somewhere else? Would you prefer to meet at my hotel?"

"No the restaurant is fine. I'll see you at eight then."

"Arrivederci"

"Yes. Arrivederci"

Elen's father stood agog in the hall.

"What was all that about?"

Elen turned and looked for an exit, but it was no use – her father was between her and the stairs so there was nothing for it but to field his interrogation.

"I'm meeting him for dinner so that he can return my phone."

Her father scratched his head.

"I don't see that you have to have dinner just to get your phone back. Sounds like you should watch this one. Be careful it's only dinner he wants."

"No Dad, it's not like that. It's just good manners, that's all."

Dad was unconvinced.

"Good manners? Just because I've waved goodbye to my hair doesn't mean my head doesn't work. No bloke offers to take a girl to a fancy restaurant just to give her phone back. This really doesn't sound like a good idea."

"Dad, it's ok. He's really nice. I met him this afternoon. He was a real gentleman."

Dad had the bit between his teeth now.

"Gentleman was he? Really? Well why doesn't he just pop

round here and bring your phone back if he's that much of a gentleman? And does this "gentleman" have a name?"

"Maybe he doesn't have a car at the moment Dad. And his name is Mac."

"No car? On the dole is he? How come he can afford to take you out if he doesn't have any money? Don't tell me he's expecting you to pay?"

"No Dad. He isn't on the dole. He has a lot of money. He's staying in a hotel in Cardiff."

"What? He's on holiday and you're the holiday fling?"

"Dad, no. He's here on business."

"What sort of business? Monkey business?"

Elen began to lose her temper.

"Look Dad. He's a businessman. He wears very expensive clothes. He has lots of money. He was very kind to me this afternoon when I fell over at the castle and I'm sure he will be a perfect gentleman tonight. It's all perfectly safe."

"Fell? What do you mean 'fell'? Are you all right? Where did you fall from?"

She sighed.

"Yes, I'm fine. I tripped up and would have fallen flat on my face if he hadn't caught me. He picked up my things and made sure I was ok. We chatted for a while and that was it. OK?"

Her father retreated.

"Oh, I see. But what about the other fella? Where was he when all this was happening?"

"Rhys? He was putting stuff back in the car."

"Well are you going out with him?"

"Who?"

"I don't know – you tell me!"

Elen felt very very tired.

"Dad I'm having dinner with Mac. I'm not going out with Rhys. We are just friends."

This seemed to pacify him for the moment. Elen lifted her bag and made her way past her father up the stairs.

"Do you want a cup of tea?"

He shouted up after her.

"Yes, please. I'll be down in a bit."

She sat on the edge of the bed. Her stomach still had butterflies the size of jumbo jets. She thought about what she had told her father. She didn't know if Mac was a businessman. He could be a film star or a drug baron for all she knew. She was presuming an awful lot of things here. Her sense of self preservation took over. She walked back down stairs. Her father was still in the kitchen. Making sure he had the door closed Elen picked up the phone.

"Rhi? It's me. I need a favour."

"Ok. But why are your whispering?"

"I don't want my dad to hear."

"So why don't you ring me on your mobile."

"I've sort of lost my mobile. But someone had found it and wants to give it back to me."

"Els, you're not making any sense here."

"Look. I met this seriously gorgeous guy today. It was really weird. I literally fell into his arms. Then I lost my phone. He found it and now he wants me to have dinner with him."

"Congratulations. What happened to bag boy then? I thought the big romantic date was today."

"The big romantic date wasn't that romantic. He isn't interested Rhi. He just wants a friend."

"Did he say that?"

"He didn't have to. He didn't make a move. We had all day together, he was really nice and I enjoyed his company but that was it."

"Did you make a move?"

"No of course I didn't."

"Wimp."

"I'm not. It just… oh never mind. Look, I need you to come to Cardiff with me tonight."

"I am going to Cardiff. With a friend."

"Friend?"

"Simon."

"Simon? Splodge? So you're on first name terms now are you? What time are you going?"

"Yes, sort of. We are going down about half eight to get there for half nine. Why?"

"That's no good. I'm meeting this guy at eight. I don't want to be there on my own. It's ok, once I've met him you can go do what ever you want, but at least I will have the excuse of meeting you if it looks dodgy."

"Ok. I'll ring Splodge."

"Thanks. I owe you one."

Elen put the phone down and breathed a sigh of relief. She didn't like taking risks. She would set up a code with Rhian. If she wasn't happy she would text her and Rhian would ring her. Then Elen could make the excuse of having to leave because her friend wasn't well or something. Annoying and embarrassing as it was, her father's third degree had made her realise she knew nothing about Mac really. And Elen wasn't into blind dates. Her father emerged with a mug of tea.

"Look, Elen. Are you sure meeting this bloke is a good idea? Do you really need your phone? Can't you get another one?"

"I can't afford another one. It's ok Dad. Rhian is coming with me. I'm not going to take any risks."

"Oh that's ok then."

She accepted the mug and sipped on the hot tea. This was most unlike her, she reflected. What was she letting herself in for?

The Caterpillar and the Hook

໔   ໖

Elen smoothed the outline of the pale pink satin against her hips. Yes, the dress had been worth the money. It fitted her like a glove, emphasising her curves without looking tarty. She played with her hair. Should she wear it up or down? Up looked older, more sophisticated, and Mac was much older than her. By how much, she wondered? She stared at her reflection in the mirror with her hair held up behind her head. One strand fell at her shoulder. Suddenly she felt vulnerable. No, she would wear it down. The elegant young woman in the mirror studied her closely, the image frightened her. She put the dress back on the hanger and selected a calf length brown fake suede skirt from the wardrobe in its place. She took a mint green polo neck jumper from the drawer and pulled a box containing her favourite green velvet boots from under the bed. She was not ready to be grown up just yet.

Her father was getting ready to go out. Saturday night was the one night of the week when he allowed himself that luxury. He met his friends at the social club, played snooker, had a game of bingo and watched the "turn". Then he came home at eleven o'clock, watched the news and went to bed. His routine was as regular as clockwork, as predictable as the sunrise over the moss glazed crags which cradled the village in their protective arms. He put on his white shirt, selected a tie from the small collection on the back of the wardrobe door, combed his hair and put on his jacket. In the hallway Elen straightened his tie and inspected his handiwork.

"Yes, you'll do."

He smiled and reached his coat out from the under stairs cupboard. He zipped up the front and turned his collar against the cold.

"Are you going to be alright?"

His question hung in the air for what seemed like an age. Elen nodded and smiled as reassuringly as she could.

"I'm a big girl now, Dad. And I won't take any chances I promise you."

"Be careful."

"I will be. I'll probably be back before you are anyway."

He nodded and kissed her cheek.

"Have a good night. Got your lucky pen?"

Her father laughed.

"Of course. I feel a big win coming on tonight. Have a good time, love."

With that he opened the front door and went out into the frosty Saturday evening.

Elen applied her make-up with care, she wanted to look nice, but not as if she had made a special effort. Then she put on her coat, picked up her car keys and headed out of the house. She was on high alert tonight. She double checked that she had enough petrol and made sure she had her AA membership card. She drove to her friend's house. For once Rhian was waiting on the doorstep with Splodge. Elen glanced at the clock. She was five minutes early. The new love of Rhian's life must be really having an effect on her, she mused. The love birds piled into the back of the car. Rhian was torn between making the most of the opportunity and finding out more about Elen's mystery man. Curiosity won.

"Well, go on then? Who's the hunk with the phone and how did it happen?"

Elen didn't want to give too much away in front of Splodge. She was very aware that he was Rhys's best friend and didn't want to cause him any pain. Besides which, there was always the possibility that he was really incredibly shy and that he did intend more than friendship. But she doubted that.

"I didn't say he was a hunk." Elen was defensive.

Rhian opened and closed her mouth without saying anything. She too, felt Splodge's presence was restricting. There was a "girlie" code. You don't discuss boys when other boys are around.

"I lost my phone earlier today, someone has found it and I'm going to pick it up. End of story."

Elen turned on the radio and headed the car towards Cardiff. Sporadic stifled giggles came from the back seat. Elen began to wonder if there had been any point whatsoever in bringing her best friend along.

"Where are you meeting the guy with your phone?"

Rhian was back in the land of the living again, if only temporarily.

"Outside the little Italian restaurant round the corner from the New Theatre."

"So what do you want us to do?"

Elen was parking the car now in the well lit multi-storey car park. She was very particular about safety and always used this car park as it had a "ladies area" close to the exit.

"If I'm at all worried I'll text you. Ring me and I'll make my excuses – say you are ill or something and that I have to leave. Then meet me outside."

Rhian nodded.

"If it's all ok I will let you know and I'll head for home. What time are you planning on leaving?"

"When they chuck us out I suppose. Two –ish?"

"Too late for me. I have dinner with my dad tomorrow."

"Oh yes, of course – it's your birthday!"

"Yes, so I really don't want a late night tonight. The meal isn't booked until two, but you know what my dad is like. He'll want to be up at the crack of dawn, just in case he isn't ready on time, then he'll be sitting in his best suit for three hours before we go."

Going out for a meal on her birthday had always been a tradition when her mother was alive. The first year after her death they had found it almost impossible to contemplate, but her father had said that her mother would be looking down on them and would be upset if they didn't carry on living normally. As the years had passed things had got easier, but it was always tinged with poignancy. They made a point, now, of asking for a table for two. Having to look at an empty chair would have been more than either of them could bear.

Elen locked the car and they began to walk towards the theatre. The city was already bustling with people. When they got to the crossroads they turned right. The little restaurant was already in view. Outside stood a tall man dressed in a long coat. Elen recognised him immediately. There was an air of confidence in the way that he stood, upright, back straight, taking up as much space as possible, assuming complete mastery of all he surveyed. As he heard their footsteps he turned towards him. Even though she had only seen him that afternoon his elegance and good looks still made Elen catch her breath.

"He's drop dead gorgeous" murmured Rhian, half to herself.

"I know." Elen heard herself reply.

Splodge was apparently oblivious to their remarks but was more concerned with Mac's coat.

"Look at that – it's real leather. Quality stuff too. You wouldn't buy that in Ponty market. That must have cost a packet."

Mac walked towards them and took Elen by the hand.

"Buono sera. Hello again. The night air has flushed your cheeks. You look radiant."

He kissed her hand softly. Elen felt her insides melt and suddenly wished she had worn the pink satin dress after all.

"This is Rhian, and Simon. My friends."

Mac kissed Rhian's hand. She flushed and giggled. Splodge scowled. Then Mac shook him by the hand with a grip that nearly severed his arm at the elbow. The younger man deferred, backed off and grinned inanely.

"Will your friends be joining us for dinner?"

"No". Elen was flustered.

"We're going clubbing. You can join us if you like."

"Thank you, but I think another time maybe."

The audience was at an end.

"See you later."

Elen waved as Rhian and Splodge turned toward the centre of town and began to walk away.

"Happy birthday for tomorrow"

Rhian shouted back as they disappeared from view.

Mac took Elen by the hand.

"It is your birthday?"

"Yes. Twenty two tomorrow."

Mac smiled.

"A beautiful butterfly – just preparing to open her wings. You have much ahead of you Elen Lloyd."

Then his tone changed.

"Your hands are cold. We had better get inside."

He opened the door and ushered her into the restaurant. Their table was upstairs, in a secluded corner, overlooking the street. The friendly waiter handed them the menu. Mac spoke to him in Italian. Then he turned to Elen.

"What would you like my dear?"

Elen ordered bruccecheta for starters and seafood linguine as a main course. Mac nodded his approval. More Italian.

"Wine?"

"No thank you, I'm driving. Just water for me please."

"In that case I won't drink either." Mac was the epitome of politeness.

"No, please. Don't abstain on my account. I really don't mind." Protested Elen.

Mac waved her worries aside.

"No, no. It is always best not to drink. I like to keep a clear head. Tonight I want to focus only on you."

Elen blushed but smiled back at him. There was an awkward silence for a few moments, then Mac produced her phone from his pocket.

"Your phone. You will see I have taken the liberty of putting my number in your address book. I hope you don't mind. I didn't want to take the risk of losing contact with you again."

Elen's heart was beating just a little too fast. She took the phone from his warm hand, thanked him and put it carefully into her bag. The waiter brought the starters. The food was delicious and soon they began to chat more comfortably. The drinks were lowered from the upper floor by a bucket, which caused much excitement from the diners. Mac wiped the edges of his mouth with his napkin.

"I have a confession"

He looked directly into Elen's eyes and the intensity was almost painful.

"Oh dear. Let's hear it then."

Elen wasn't sure if he was joking with her or not.

"Today was not the first time I have seen you."

Elen didn't know how to take this. What on earth did he mean? Had he been stalking her? She felt a tinge of panic and her hand instinctively reached into her bag for her phone.

"You misunderstand."

His voice was calm, with no hint of threat.

"I saw you in a dream."

What? Was he spinning her a line? Surely such tactics went out as soon as boys got out of junior school. Although she did remember being impressed at age fourteen when Bryan Evans said she looked like an angel. She wasn't quite so impressed she recalled five minutes later when he tried to put his tongue down her throat. Yuk!

Mac sensed her mood.

"Let me explain. I was in a car crash some months ago. Nothing so very serious but I lost consciousness."

Elen studied his face, but could find no trace of deceit.

"Go, on."

"While I was 'out of it' I had what I suppose you would call an out of body experience."

"You saw yourself?"

"Not exactly. I had a vision."

"What sort of vision? Blinding white light? A tunnel?"

"No. Nothing like that really. It was most strange, and yet at the same time I felt completely at peace. As though I was meant to be there."

His tone had hooked her in. She nodded. Elen wanted desperately to believe such things were possible. Since the death of her mother she needed to feel that there was somewhere else to go and that her mother was at peace. Mac had her full attention now, and he knew it.

"I was driving near the base of the valley. I knew the road, but now, I could not tell you where it was. I could smell pine trees. It was so vivid. The road followed the course of the river. I decided to drive up the mountain just to see what was there.

"It was a steep climb. The road twisted and turned but kept on going. Forever upwards. Everything was very quiet, very still. I was very cold. I had no idea where I was, but everything was somehow familiar. When I got to the top I could see a vast plateau to one side. I began to scramble down the mountain. The rocks were sharp under my feet. I walked for an age and eventually came to the base of the mountain by the side of the river."

Elen sat in silence, completely captivated. Mac pressed his fingertips together, looking at her intently, gauging her reaction.

"There was a small boat tied up at the side of the river with an ancient almost toothless old man standing beside it. His clothes seemed to be made of dust. He gave me the rope from the boat and then he disappeared before my very eyes. I felt no alarm. I got into the boat and let it take me downstream.

"I came to a beautiful city. There was a huge harbour, with vast ocean going ships. I walked through a villa and into a smaller harbour filled with yachts. I cannot sail, but I went aboard and suddenly we were making our way across an azure sea. I say we, I saw no-one. The boat propelled itself."

Elen felt a shiver go through her. They had finished their meal now.

"I slept. I do not know for how long I slept. When I awoke the boat was anchored on a pretty island. Someone was there, beckoning to me. He led me on board a jet. I saw no crew."

"Were you afraid?" Elen felt this was all very spooky and she was more than a little uncomfortable.

"No. I felt completely safe. At peace. I was where I was meant to be. The plane touched down near a wood. I walked through it and into a castle. I could see every detail. I went in and saw an old man sitting on a chair. Then I saw the most beautiful woman I had ever seen in my life. She was perfect. I walked towards her and she stumbled, her ivory skin as soft as swan's down against my cheek as she fell into my arms."

"What happened next"

Elen had not yet realised that he was talking about her.

"I awoke and found myself in hospital. And the girl of my dreams was gone."

"Ah. I've read a lot about out of body experiences when people are close to death, but I've never heard of anything quite like what to describe. What did you make of it?"

"I dismissed it as a fantasy created by my fevered brain. Until today."

"Today? What happened today?"

Mac took a deep breath and wrapped his fingers around Elen's hand.

"Today, I found my castle and suddenly there you were, exactly as I remembered you, and just as in my dream you fell straight into my arms."

Elen was completely taken aback. She released her hand from his grip and stared at him in alarm. Was the man mad?

"Me? Are you sure?"

"Oh yes, I would have known you anywhere. Today, however, you did not disappear. You were flesh and blood. And even when you left, there behind you was your phone. A calling card from my Cinderella."

He was serious. She was sure of it. Elen felt the smoothness of the metal of her phone against her fingers. Had fate really caused her to leave her phone behind so that they would meet again? It was an intriguing idea. A thrilling one, to be honest. She decided to keep an open mind. They left the restaurant and Mac walked her to her car.

"Thank you for a lovely evening."

"The pleasure was all mine. When will I see you again, my beautiful Elena?"

She hesitated.

"I don't know. I will ring you tomorrow."

"That is all I can ask for. I shall await your call. Have a wonderful birthday. I shall speak to you in the morning."

"Yes. That would be nice."

"Elen?"

"Yes?"

"This is presumptuous. But my heart is longing. May I kiss you?"

Her legs turned to marshmallow. He held her face gently as the warmth of his lips met hers. The kiss was soft but with a promise of passion.

He pulled away.

"Good night, cara mia. How do you say that in your Welsh?"

"Nos da fy nghariad."

Mac tried the words out, wrapping his tongue around them. Then he laughed.

"Well, 'Nos da' my lovely vision. Don't dissolve before my eyes again."

With that she got into her car. Dissolve, she thought! Her whole inner being seemed to be dissolving, into a sugary sweet syrup. She turned the key, waved, and drove out of the car park.

She parked the car outside her house and picked up her phone. There was a text from Rhian asking if everything was ok. Elen texted back.

HOME NOW, EVERYTHING IS WONDERFUL

What a very strange and very wonderful evening. Was he right about fate lending a hand? She wanted to believe. Could this handsome man truly be her Prince Charming? Was this it? Was destiny really calling her? Did happiness ever after have her name on it? She brushed her hair, her eyes alighting once more on her mother's photograph. Tenderly she traced the outline of the butterflies with a finger. What would her mother have made of all this? She was nervous, fearful, but tingling with excitement and anticipation. What would she say to him tomorrow? She put down the hairbrush and prepared to go to bed. Tomorrow would bring what ever it would.

Happy Birthday

Rhian was on the phone long before Elen had even got out of bed.

"What happened? All I got was a text saying everything was fine and that you had gone home."

Elen felt the heat in her cheeks. Her head was still somewhere else and she had hardly slept a wink thinking about Mac and also about Rhys.

"And happy birthday to you, best friend."

She avoided answering the question.

"Oh, sorry. Happy birthday. I'll be over later with your pressie. Look, I'm going mad with curiosity here."

"And you know what curiosity did…"

"Miaow! I'll take the risk. WHAT HAPPENED?"

Elen sunk back in her pillow and basked in the memory of the previous evening.

"It was wonderful."

"What was? Did you go home with him? He didn't come home with you did he?"

"NO! Oh Rhi, don't be silly. You know I don't move that fast."

"Dearest best friend, if you don't start moving soon what's left won't be worth moving for!"

"Oh come on. We had a lovely meal and he was really romantic."

"Like how?"

"Like he said he had seen me in a dream."

"Pass the sick bag. And you believed him?"

"Yes. No. I don't know. I think I did at the time. He was such a gentleman. He even asked my permission to kiss me."

"He did what?"

"Asked if he could kiss me. No one has ever done that before."

"No one has ever done that to me either. I don't usually wait to be asked."

Elen laughed.

"He made me feel special. Treasured. Like a delicate piece of bone china. When he held me he was so gentle, as if he was afraid I would break."

Rhian made a strange gurgling noise down the phone.

"Ok, so what happened next?"

"Nothing."

"Nothing?"

"He kissed me…."

"Tongues?"

"Rhian! He kissed me goodnight, saw me safely into my car and blew me a kiss as I drove off."

"You drove off?"

"Well yes. Of course."

There was silence at the end of the phone.

"Rhi? Are you still there?"

"Yes. I was just thinking what I would have done if I had got Mr sex-on-legs champing at the bit. I don't think it would have included driving off and leaving him standing in a freezing car park!"

"Rhi, I'm not like you. I don't want to take it any faster than this. It was, well, perfect."

"You're being boring again."

"Maybe. It's how I want it to be."

"Ok. Have it your way. Or don't have it at all as it were. When are you seeing him again?"

"I don't know."

"You don't know? Els, don't you know ANYTHING about dating blokes?"

"What do you mean?"

"You always fix the next date before you say goodnight. You don't ever, and I mean EVER get yourself into a situation where he says he will call you. Because he never will. They don't. If you don't fix a time and place that's the end of it."

There was a pause. Elen felt slightly sick,

"You mean I've blown it?"

"Possibly. How keen was he?"

Elen wasn't sure.

"Keen. I think. I don't know. I can't judge these things."

"How keen are you?"

This was an even more difficult question.

"I like him. I like him at lot. But I still really like Rhys."

"Did he make a move yesterday?"

"Who?"

"Bag boy."

Elen could hear the irritation in her friend's voice. It was all so easy for Rhian. She didn't agonise over things the way that Elen did. She flitted from man to man like a butterfly from flower to flower (ok, maybe more like a hippopotamus from lake to lake), and if it bothered her that her relationships never lasted she didn't let it show. Not even to Elen.

"No. I thought he was going to, but then he seemed to get cold feet. Coming back in the car was awful. You could have cut the atmosphere with a knife. I like him, but I don't think he likes me. Not in that way, anyway."

"That's men for you. Just when you think you've got them

figured they do something completely alien. They really are a different species."

"I guess."

At this point the door bell rang. Elen looked at the bedside clock. It was only 9.30. Who came calling at that hour on a Sunday?

"Got to go, someone at the door,"

Elen put down the phone. She could hear her father moving around down stairs.

"Elen!"

She put on her dressing gown and went down to see what the commotion was.

"Look!"

Her father was indicating a huge bouquet of red roses on the hall table.

"It's Sunday. They don't deliver flowers on a Sunday."

She was baffled.

"They came by special courier. Must have cost a fortune." Her father was equally confused. Elen opened the small envelope that was attached to the flowers.

Happy Birthday my beautiful Vision.
Thank you for a wonderful evening.
Mac x

She put the card back in the envelope. Her father was hovering anxiously.

"Well? Who are they from?"

"A friend."

"Friends don't send expensive flowers by special delivery. Rhian would never do anything like that."

"A male friend."

"That boy you went out with yesterday afternoon."

"No. The guy I had dinner with last night."

She could see the alarm in her father's face. She moved quickly to allay his fears.

"It's ok dad. Nothing happened. We had a nice meal, he walked me to my car and that was that. These flowers are completely out of the blue."

"What did he say on the card?"

"Happy Birthday."

Elen deftly picked up the small envelope and put it into her dressing gown pocket.

"Right. Breakfast."

"Oh I completely forgot. Happy Birthday, my darling."

"Thanks Dad"

Elen was grateful for the change of subject. She opened the kitchen door and busied herself with tea and toast. She was aware that her hands were shaking slightly. What on earth was Mac thinking of? Red roses? It was too grand a gesture after just one date. Was it even a date? She didn't know what to think. The roses were beautiful, lovely. They were just the sort of romantic gesture she had always dreamed of. So why did she feel so uncomfortable? She ate her toast in silence and then went upstairs to take a shower and get dressed. Her phone was still on the bedside table. It registered two new text messages. She decided to take a shower first. If the messages were from Mac she didn't want to respond to them just yet. She pulled the comb through her wet hair and looked again at the phone. Three messages now. Nothing for it. She would have to look at them.

The first one was from Rhys.

"Happy Birthday. Hope you like the book. Have a great day. Rhys x"

She had forgotten about her present from Rhys. She felt a pang of anguish. If only he had at least shown some interest yesterday she wouldn't be in this predicament. The second message was from Rhian.

"Happy birthday. Have you heard from lover boy yet?"

The third message was from Mac. Elen hesitated before she opened it. She took a deep breath.

"Wishing a lovely lady a wonderful birthday. May I see you again? Please? Mac x"

Why did he have to be so romantic? Why did he have to do everything right?

Home from Home

≈ ≪

Carla collected her luggage and walked towards the exit door. She was met by a tall thin man in a khaki coloured overcoat. Rain had drenched what remained of his black hair and fogged up his silver rimmed glasses.

"Miss Theodoro?"

"Yes."

"Phil Tomlinson, of South Wales Executive Lettings."

"Ah, Mr Tomlinson. You have the keys to the apartments?"

The man touched his black leather briefcase and nodded.

"Yes, it's all in here. I have the paperwork ready. Would you like to go over it here or would you prefer to go back to my office?"

"It's been a long day, Mr Tomlinson. Can we grab a table over there and complete the paperwork. I'm eager to settle in."

They sat down at a small round table in the lounge area and the man took out a set of forms from his briefcase. He seemed overly anxious.

"Here we are. The forms are exactly as I copied to you last week. Terms of the lease an initial two months with an option of a monthly extension with six weeks notice."

Carla read through the forms carefully.

"Everything seems to be in order."

She smiled.

"If you could just sign here please."

He handed her a ball point pen. She waved it aside and took out an elegant gold fountain pen from her bag.

"You are new with the firm I understand."

She signed the papers. For the first time her companion smiled.

"Yes. You are my first client. I've gone over everything very carefully. I wanted to make sure everything is just right. The apartments are in an exclusive development overlooking Cardiff bay. It has its own secure car park. Oh, you will need a key fob to open the security gates. Here are the keys. Two for each property as requested."

Carla handed the papers back and put the keys and the fobs into her handbag.

"Would you like me to accompany you to the property to make sure that everything is in order? I was there earlier, but .."

She cut him short.

"That won't be necessary. Thank you Mr Tomlinson. It has been a pleasure doing business with you."

She stood up, collected her baggage and walked towards the door.

"Can I give you a lift, or call you a taxi?"

"No thank you."

She walked out of the door. Philip Tomlinson hurriedly collected his papers, checked through them briefly and put them back into his case. That had gone well, he thought. Strange woman. But then, continentals have different ways, he reasoned.

Carla took her mobile phone out of her bag.

"G? It's me. I have the keys to the flat. Now where are you?"

"I have just parked the car. In the short stay area in front of the airport. The deep blue Mercedes."

"Got you."

She snapped her phone shut and walked towards the car. A tall elegant man opened the door and stepped out. He took her bags and placed them in the boot of the car, then he opened the passenger door for her. He walked around the car and got in at the driver's side. The door made a reassuring click as it closed. He leaned over to her and stroked her cheek. Then he took hold of her head with one hand and kissed her firmly on the mouth. His other hand wandered along her thigh. She pulled away.

"Not here."

"I have missed you Carla."

"I have missed you too, but we agreed — no passion in public."

"No-one here knows us."

"I don't care. Wait until we get to the flat."

He sighed and started the engine. She laughed.

"What's so funny?"

"You. You are like a teenage boy."

"You make me feel like a teenager."

She held his gaze as he put the car into gear. Then they sped off into the darkness.

Lunch

෧   ෧

Elen lay back on the bed and drifted into sleep. Her dreams were tangled. At one point she was kissing Rhys and then he turned into Mac. Then she was a little girl again, falling over on the beach and running to her mother for comfort. She awoke with a start and looked at the clock. It was time to get ready to go to lunch. Her father shouted from downstairs.

"I'm ready now, love. What time do you want to leave? We don't want to leave it too late. You never know how the traffic is going to be on a Sunday."

"Yes you do" she thought to herself.
"There will be next to no traffic at all and we will be sitting in the lounge like lemons waiting for our table to be ready."

She articulated none of this of course. Instead she shouted down sweetly

"I'll be down in a few minutes Dad. Just drying my hair. Why don't you make yourself a cup of tea while you are waiting?"

She finished her hair, put on her Sunday best dress and walked down to the kitchen.

"You look lovely. If only your mother could see you, she would have been so proud."

He had spoken from the heart but his words hit a tender spot that never quite seemed to heal. Elen looked away, unable to bear the closeness. Then they made sure all the windows were closed, locked the doors and went out to lunch.

It was her father's favourite restaurant, with its Sunday lunch carvery. He always made a big fuss about choosing what he wanted.

"Oh, the lamb looks nice. What do you think, Elen? But the turkey looks lovely too. Spoilt for choice."

Elen nodded and then he chose as he always did, roast beef and Yorkshire pudding. Elen decided on salmon. Any other day it would have seemed like an occasion. Maybe it was the food the night before, maybe it was just that Elen was growing older, or more sophisticated. She couldn't help but notice that the potatoes were frozen, not fresh and that the vegetables seemed to have been stewing for ages. She had wanted to go to a lovely little restaurant a couple of miles down the road. She had been there once for a friend's birthday and their Sunday lunch was really good. But her father had always gone to the same place and the thought of going elsewhere sent him into a flat panic.

"Do they do roast beef there?"

"Yes Dad. They do."

"Ah, but do they do apple pie and custard?"

"I don't know, but I had crème brulee and it was delicious."

"Oh I don't know love. I'm not really fussed on this foreign stuff. Best go to the Crown eh? We know what we will get there. We don't want a disappointment on your birthday."

Elen had nodded but part of her was screaming

"Yes, I know what we will have. We will have the same thing as we have had for the last five years. How about a little unpredictability?"

But what came out was

"Yes, I suppose you are right."

He wiped the last traces of apple pie and custard from his mouth and announced

"Well, shall we be off then? "

Elen went to her room as her father slept off his lunch. She looked at Rhys's present on her dressing table. She picked it up but a surge of pain and panic hit her and she replaced it again. Why was it so painful to think about Rhys? She wished she could sort out her feelings for him. She wished she could read his feelings for her! She went over each moment of their outing on Saturday in her mind. She had been so sure that he was interested. Maybe she was just listening to Rhian too much. Rhian thought EVERY guy was interested. No, she decided, if he had felt that way he would have made a move, which he hadn't, so that was the end of that. Now she had to sort out what to do about Mac. He really was dishy, and so, what was the word, 'debonair'. He was just like a character out of a film. Everything, from the way he dressed, to the way his dark wavy hair fell boyishly into his eyes, to the way his eyes crinkled when he smiled – it was all perfect. Was he too good to be true? When he phoned, *if* he phoned, she would keep herself under complete control. She found the way her thoughts raced when she was with him alarming. It was almost as if she was under some sort of spell. No, she had to get a grip. Show him who was boss. He would have to pursue her, she was not going to do the chasing. That was how it was going to be. Definitely. She was strong. In control. Her musing was interrupted by her phone. It was Mac.

"Happy birthday."

"Thank you" she replied, unable to stop herself from smiling.

"Did you like the flowers?"

"Yes, thank you."

She had the giggles, despite her resolve.

"I wondered if you were free tomorrow evening? We have a lot to talk about."

"I think I could arrange that" she answered almost hugging herself with delight.

"I have just moved into my new apartment. So, I would like to cook for you. A proper Italian meal."

Elen was taken aback. He could cook? Tall, dark, handsome, rich, romantic *and* he cooked? She wondered if he liked poetry, listened to the words of songs and didn't make a mess in the bathroom too? How could she refuse?

"What time?"

"About eight o'clock? I shall give you the address."

Elen took down the address. It was in a very expensive part of Cardiff, on the bay, overlooking the estuary. Very impressive.

"When you get to the gates, phone me, I will get the porter to open them for you. Drive into the car park then come around to the first building on your right. I will buzz you up. Fourth floor. I will be waiting for you."

"Ok. I'll see you then."

"Oh, I shall see you before then I think."

She was confused.

"You will? How?"

"In my dreams, my little one, in my dreams."

Elen blushed as she put down the phone. She just *had* to phone Rhian.

"Rhi – he's asked me over to his place for dinner. He wants to cook for me?"

Rhian was barely awake. But then it was only mid afternoon and it was Sunday.

"Who? Bag boy or the incredible hunk?"

Elen laughed.

"Mac. He wants to cook me an authentic Italian meal.

What do you think of that? He cooks!"

Rhian was less than impressed.

"You can always get a take away. Are you going to get some authentic latin loving? That's the real question!"

Elen was aghast. She hadn't thought of that. Was he just luring her back to his place with only one thing on the agenda? Did he think that cooking her a meal would entitle him to dessert? Maybe she should ring him and arrange to meet somewhere more public. Rhian laughed out loud at her friend's fears.

"Elen – grow up, will you? You're twenty two – you're a woman. He's a man. If it happens it happens! If you don't want it then you can make it clear during the meal and if he's everything you say he is then he'll wait. Although why you would *want* to wait is beyond me. He's gorgeous."

"I can't Rhi. I just have to have a real emotional connection. I need to feel safe."

Rhian sighed.

"Yeah, I know. It's the way you are. But be careful – you spend so much time living in the past and living in the future that you are forgetting to live in the here and now! I'm sure that when you are in your eighties you won't be saying – oh I wish I'd had less fun! Let go a bit. Live! It's what you're here for. If it isn't fun why do it?"

It was a difficult question to answer. Thoughts of "duty" and "doing what's right" came into Elen's head but she knew that wouldn't persuade her outgoing friend. Maybe she was right. Maybe she should let go. She couldn't remember the last time she had really had fun. Not without feeling guilty that she should be somewhere else – or doing something 'worthwhile'. She would make her intentions clear, but if it happened it happened. Maybe. Maybe not yet. Maybe definitely not yet. The caterpillar wasn't ready to shed its protective skin just yet.

Valley's Telegraph

⤳ ⤶

Splodge put down eight cans on beer on the kitchen table and sat down. Rhys looked at him in bewilderment.

"What's this? It's early – even for you!"

His friend looked awkward. He leaned over and opened a can. He passed it to Rhys.

"What? It's not even lunchtime. What's going on?"

"Drink"

"No, I don't drink during the day. I shall be asleep all afternoon if I do."

"So?"

"So I've got an assignment to finish. It's a reading week not a holiday. Si, it's important. It's an intensive year. You know that."

Splodge put the can into Rhys's hand and pressed his fingers around it. Then, with more than the required element of melodrama leaned over and muttered

"You need it."

"I do?"

"Yes."

"Why?"

Splodge looked at his feet, then out of the window and then back at Rhys.

"Look mate, I know you've got the hots for Rhian's mate..."

"Elen?"

"Yeah – Elen. Look, it's like this. Rhi and I were out last Saturday night and she was meeting someone."

"Why didn't you tell me last Saturday night?"

"She said it was a one off. She was getting her phone from a guy who had found it."

"And?"

"I've just spoken to Rhi. She says Elen is going to meet him again tomorrow."

Rhys tried hard not to let the emotion show in his face. He felt utterly drained. He sat in silence and swigged the can of beer. Splodge opened another one for himself.

"Who is he? Anyone we know?"

Splodge wiped the beer from his upper lip.

"I don't think so. Foreign guy. Tall, very smart."

Rhys looked up.

"Dark hair? Sharp suit?"

Splodge looked surprised.

"Yeah. Lot older than us. Looked very well off, very 'suave' Rhian said."

"I know him. Well, at least, I've met him. Greasy dago."

"I think he was Italian actually"

"Same difference."

Rhys tipped the remainder of the can down his throat and opened another one. That was the end of the assignment for today. He stared gloomily at the row of empty cans on the table.

"Women" said Splodge.

"Yeah" Rhys nodded.

"You wanna watch the rugby from Saturday? "

"Yeah – why not?"

Splodge handed Rhys a disk, Rhys turned on the TV and Splodge opened the last remaining can.

Plans are Laid

❧ ❧

It was 6.30 am. Mac had been up for ages already. He had a lot to do. He sipped at black coffee as he checked the website again for the number. There it was. His eyes gleamed as he flicked through the images in the on-line gallery. Yes, perfect. He rang the number. A man's voice answered, a cultured obviously artistic accent.

"Hello, am I speaking to Mr Nowakowski. I'm interested in one of your artworks."

He paused and listened.

"Yes. The stained glass magical castle one. Yes, Castell Coch – I thought it looked like it. Good. Can you deliver?"

Mac gave his credit card details and the delivery address. Then he turned his attention to the caterers. The evening had to be just perfect. He cast his eye over the bedroom. Would the evening get that far, he wondered? No matter, best to be prepared. He knew exactly what he wanted. He had seen it in the fashionable quarter of Cardiff just days before. He grabbed his car keys and briefcase as he headed for the door. Even the early morning drizzle could not dampen his spirits today. The deal was going well, he had everything in place and now he had met the girl from his vision. He was listening to his dreams just as his grandmother had told him to. With a frown, he remembered her warning about a dangerous woman. Would it be wise not to mix business with pleasure? Mac had always been a pleasure seeker and had become expert at juggling his life to accommodate both. Elen was an innocent. There was no danger here.

He telephoned Carla. She was already at the office, efficient as usual. He barked his orders as he drove along the dual carriageway. He tapped his fingers with annoyance on the steering wheel. Brits drive so slowly. No wonder they never seem to achieve anything. His mind flitted back to his preparations for dinner with Elen that night. The thrill of the chase, there was nothing like it. Mac felt alive when he was wooing a woman. Winning her over, gaining her confidence and the anticipation of the eventual dénouement − even clinching a major deal didn't give him the same buzz. He enjoyed the quickening of his heartbeat as he thought about the events to come. He had felt that way once about Kata. But now the rhythm of their life together had settled down to a dull steady beat which did nothing to excite him. She was still beautiful, yes − and she could still ignite his passion − but he didn't have to try for it. Everything cloys with familiarity he concluded. He pulled himself out of his thoughts and began to mentally prepare for the days business. That was what he was getting paid for, after all.

Carla picked up the telephone.

"Mr Maconi's office"

Her faced softened.

"Hello. Yes, I'm well. No, he's out on location for the next few hours. The accommodation is fine, well appointed. I've taken a smaller apartment in the same block − one has to keep up appearances!"

She looked at the ceiling, and then out of the window.

"Do you now? Well, you will have to explain that to me in person…"

She played with her hair as she talked. Out of the corner of her eye she spotted Mac parking his car outside. Her tone changed.

"No. He's back. The deal is going well. I expect it will all be sewn up in the next two weeks. Then just a couple of months to oversee things. There are one or two on the board who are a bit 'anti' but I'm sure they can be won over. Give him his due, Mac is good at that. Yes, that too."

She laughed.

"See you soon"

She put down the phone, straightened her jacket and returned her gaze to the files on her desk. Mac opened the door.

"Carla, I have an assignment for you."

She looked up from her work with an amused gleam in her eyes.

"Sounds interesting?"

Mac sat down on the edge of her desk, swinging his legs forward towards her. He waved a file and a photograph at her.

"Phillip Fisher. He's pretty much key to us getting the deal. I think he's double dealing. I need you to find out."

She nodded; no emotion betrayed and took the file from Mac's hand. She flicked through it.

"It certainly looks suspicious. What do you have in mind?"

Mac handed her a business card.

"This is the contact details for a private detective – she comes highly recommended. I want you to meet with her this evening to discuss the next step. I know that Fisher is having dinner with a lady friend tonight – the restaurant address is in the file. I've booked a table for you both. You can observe while you chat."

He stood up. Carla frowned.

"Why do you need a private detective? It seems to me that

you know pretty much everything about him anyway?"

Mac flicked a strand of heavily waxed hair out of his eyes.

"Not enough. I need someone with the time and energy to dig deeper. This guy is up to something. He's been blocking our deal all along the way. Something just doesn't feel right. I need to know what he's up to and who I'm up against."

He handed her an envelope.

"Here's some cash to go buy yourself something pretty for this evening and get your hair fixed or whatever. You can take the afternoon to do whatever you feel is necessary. When you go over to say hello to Mr Fisher I want you to knock his socks off. That shouldn't be too hard for you, now should it?"

He flashed that broad smile again. Perfect teeth, perfectly white.

New Wings

❧ ❦

With some trepidation Elen negotiated her way around the badly sign-posted traffic system of Cardiff Bay. It must have been designed by an engineer, she decided. It assumed that you knew which direction you were going in before you got to the road, and therefore didn't need to be told which lane you needed until just after you had got into the wrong one at the next set of traffic lights. She indicated and waited for someone to let her in. The young man in the baseball cap in the car to her rear was not amused. She waited. The horn sounded again behind her. Oh dear. He looked really annoyed. Elen had visions of him striding out of the car in a full attack of road rage. Fortunately a lorry driver took pity on her and allowed her out into the right lane. She could feel the perspiration on her brow. She hated driving to new places. She usually took someone with her to navigate, but it wasn't really appropriate tonight. Finally she could see the property development in front of her. Century Wharf. It looked very exclusive. She drove up to the gate and stopped the car, being careful to turn off the engine before she picked up her phone.

"Hello, Mac – it's Elen"

The gates swung open. She drove through them, jumping nervously when they closed smoothly behind her. The parking spaces were clearly marked. Her stomach was already in knots.

Tonight she had chosen to wear the pink satin dress. She had kept her coat on so that her father did not see it as she left the house. She had even told him that she might be staying at Rhian's that night. What was she thinking of?

In the flat, Mac surveyed the scene with satisfaction. The caterers had done well. The maple table was adorned with a white cloth, and in the centre was a crystal vase bearing a single red rose – exactly as he had asked for. The meal was ready prepared in the kitchen. A simple starter, an elegant main course, that wouldn't spoil too much if they took their time, and an extravagant dessert. All taken out of their containers and tweaked just enough to look home made. He had a bottle of champagne on ice – yes, she was driving, but he was hoping that she wouldn't be driving home until morning – and sparkling water – just in case she was adamant. It wasn't gentlemanly to insist. And besides, he was in no rush. The longer it took the more interesting it became. He climbed the spiral staircase to the bedroom. The new pale pink sheets were sprinkled with rose petals. Candles were strategically placed around the room. He was ready. Now where was she?

The door bell rang. Right on cue. Mac checked his reflection in the hall mirror before answering the door. His hair was slicked back, but a strand or two had made their way Bryan Ferry fashion across his dark eyes. His collar was tie-less and the linen shirt slightly crumpled with the sleeves rolled up to the elbow – after all, he had been slaving away in a hot kitchen for hours now hadn't he? With a well rehearsed smile he opened the door. The sight took his breath away. Elen, with the soft satin caressing each curve, her eyes bright, her skin glowing – Mac was lost in admiration. He took her hand and drew her to him. Then he kissed her mouth, softly at first then harder as he held her against him. He was acutely aware of the silkiness of her skin, her sweet perfume, and the supple lines of her body.

He wanted her. But he would have to wait. He knew better than to rush things. He pulled away and looked into her eyes. "My lovely Elen. You have never looked more beautiful. You are a vision. You are stunning."

Elen blushed, turned her eyes to the floor, then she lifted them again searching the huge dark eyes before her to try to gauge his intent. He was so handsome, so manly. There was nothing indecisive about Mac. He knew exactly where he was going and how he was going to get there. He had control, he had power. It made Elen both nervous and strangely reassured. She did not have to take decisions with Mac around. He could take care of everything. Her finger traced along his heavy brow line, stroked the slight stubble on his cheek and ran along his firm jaw. He smiled. He led her into the lounge. It was stylish. The light wood blocked floor was adorned with a large off white rug. It was flanked on two sides by soft leather cream sofas. She sat down while Mac busied himself in the kitchen. A maple table with four chairs was at the far end of the room. On it was a small vase with a single red rose. Elen smiled and hugged herself. This was perfect.

Mac brought out the first course and ordered her to sit. He offered her wine, but she declined, so he poured cool mineral water into one of the elegant glasses. He placed the food in front of her. Toasted bread with tomatoes and anchovies. It looked delicious.

"What is it called?" she asked.

"Bruschetta Pomodoro e Acciughe" he replied with a smile.

"Which is?"

"Bruschetta with marinated tomatoes and anchovies. Try it."

She followed his lead, raising the substantial morsel to her lips. The salty taste of the anchovies contrasted perfectly with the acid of the tomatoes. It was delightful. Her eyes widened with surprise. Was there no end to Macs' talents? He smiled at her as she ate never taking his eyes off her for a second. She enjoyed his attentiveness. She had never had anyone pay quite so much attention to her. It was an unfamiliar feeling which she couldn't quite put a name to. It made her feel good – worthy – somehow. Mac reached out and stroked her arm.

"Good?"

"Wonderful. Where did you learn to cook like that?"

"At my grandmothers' knee. Bibi is a very good cook."

"Bibi?" Elen wondered if this was his wife – or one of his children. Mac laughed.

"Bibi is my grandmother. You would like her. She is a real character. She grew up as a real Romany gypsy on the road in a wooden caravan. She didn't settle down until she was in her fifties and even now she is always up in the hills. Even sleeps up there sometimes when she's out collecting herbs for her potions. She bakes bread with secret herbs for the locals then reads their leaves. Everyone knows Bibi. Half the village is in awe of her and the other half is terrified of her!"

Elen's head tilted to one side. She could see the pride in his eyes when he talked about his grandmother.

"Do her predictions come true?"

Mac nodded seriously.

"Always. I learnt a lot of things growing up with her. She taught me to trust my instincts. She has never been wrong about anything like that. It's almost as though she can reach out and touch the future."

"And did she say anything about you working in Wales?"

Elen was as keen to know if there were any predictions for this possible romance.

"She told me to listen to my dreams. I saw you in my

123

dream, so I'm following that. I was meant to meet you. I'm sure of that."

Elen felt a prickle of excitement rise through her. Mac lost his serious expression and sauntered back to the kitchen to get the main course. And what a piece de résistance it turned out to be. Veal in a white wine sauce with cream and mushrooms. It was so tender it almost melted on her tongue. The side vegetables were fresh and crunchy. Elen had to admit it was the most delicious meal she had ever had. Mac watched her enjoying her food with obvious delight. Not for him the stick thin super efficient women who survived on a lettuce leaf. He believed that all appetites were connected and viewed Elen's as a very good sign in deed. He tried once more to tempt her with wine. Again she refused. He poured more water for both himself and Elen. Mac rarely drank in company. Alcohol has the tendency to make one unguarded and for someone who played the game with his cards as close to his chest as Mac an unguarded moment could not be afforded.

Mac chatted about his childhood. He told her that his mother had died when he was a small boy, and that his father died not long after. He was brought up on the shores of Lake Garda by his Spanish grandmother and his aging grandfather. They adored each other despite an age gap of more than twenty years. His grandfather had only recently died and Mac was still very close to Bibi, visiting her religiously at least once a month. Elen thought it slightly odd that when Mac returned to Italy he visited his grandmother but not always his children. She was on the point of questioning this but decided that the whole business of his estranged wife and family was not a subject she really wanted to delve into. Mac disappeared once more to return with dessert. A light as a feather panacotta served with a mouth watering raspberry coulis. The man was a marvel.

"How do you make this? It's lovely. It's so light."

Mac touched his nose and laughed.

"Family secret. If could tell you, but then you would never be able to leave the room."

They both giggled. Not a sip of wine had touched their lips but they were both intoxicated by each other. Mac watched her eyes, taking in every detail of her expressions. She was shy, but slowly coming out of her shell. She was so naïve, a tender sleeping flower just waiting for the right man to awaken her. And Mac felt sure that he was the right man. He put his hands together, and then slotted his fingers between each hand as he raised them to his chin. He watched Elen as she finished her dessert. She was so fresh, innocent and lovely. He sunk his teeth into his knuckle. She would be worth waiting for.

All of this was so new to Elen. Suddenly she was taken out of her drab valleys existence and whisked into a world made for glamorous women, where elegant men like Mac gazed attentively into their eyes. The flat was so understatedly slick. Everything, from the butter soft leather of the sofa to the superb food spoke of class. She was nervous but Mac continued to put her at her ease, coaxing the butterfly out of her chrysalis. He knew exactly what he was doing, which was a bit daunting, but he made her feel safe. She felt as though she was the only woman in the world – maybe apart from his Grandmother, Bibi – but he viewed her in an entirely different way – and surely any man who could be so devoted to an old woman was capable of great love. She smiled at him. This was all so scary, but it felt right. Was this the great adventure she had always dreamt of?

Mac cleared up the dishes and suggested they retire to one of the sofas. Elen smoothed out the creases in her dress as she awaited his return. From behind the second sofa she could see a large package wrapped in brown paper. Mac stood at the doorway, aware that she had noticed it.

"Ah, you have found my little surprise"

Elen was flustered. She hadn't meant to be nosy.

"What? No – that is I was just curious. Everything in here is so pristine – I just wondered what the package was."

Mac moved the sofa and pulled the package out.

"I was looking for some artwork for the flat. I hate the bland nondescript stuff they put in these places. And I found this."

Delicately he removed the wrapping to reveal an exquisite piece of stained glass. It was a picture – the candle light from the table shone through it and gave it a magical quality. Elen recognised the scene immediately.

"It's Castell Coch!"

"Do you like it?"

"Like it? I love it. Look at the detail – the butterflies around the border – like the ones on the wall around the banqueting room. The way the light shines through it. It comes alive. It's wonderful. Where did you get it?"

Mac turned the work so that the light changed it once more. It really did seem to come to life as the light passed through it in different directions. You felt that you could almost walk into it. Mac watched the fascination in the young woman's face. Now he would play his trump card.

"It is for you. Happy Birthday."

Elen was overwhelmed.

"But I can't accept this. It must have cost a fortune. You already gave me flowers. This is too much."

"Nothing is too much for you. Don't you understand Elen? I fell in love with the girl in my dream and when I met her in the flesh I fell in love with her all over again."

He drew her closer tangling his fingers in her dark hair as he softly kissed her neck. He breathed in deeply, inhaling her perfume as if he was drinking in her very essence. He was so very gentle but Elen could sense the passion raging inside him. It excited and frightened her at the same time. He was a man, a real man, not a fumbling boy. What was it that Rhian had said?

"You're a woman – he's a man. If it happens – it happens."

His hand dropped to her back. She felt his fingers slowly unzipping her dress as he nuzzled her neck. His breath was warm on her skin. She was so aware of him. The heat from his body. The pressure of his thigh against hers. She felt as if she was drowning. Suddenly panic rose through her. She tried to fight it. His hand was in her hair pulling her towards him. His mouth against hers. His tongue brushing her lips. He eased the strap of her dress over her shoulder sliding his fingers down towards her breast. Elen fought with herself trying to let go. Mac sensed her nervousness.

"Hey, it's all right. We don't have to do anything you are not ready for. I'm going crazy for you – but I can wait. I don't intend to let you slip out of my fingers."

He replaced the strap and redid the zip. Elen felt foolish.

"No, its ok."

Mac smiled and stroked her cheek.

"No, it isn't. You aren't ready to take that step yet. It doesn't matter how long it takes. We will wait. You will know when you want to. And so will I. And tonight you don't."

Elen felt both relieved and miserable.

"I'm sorry."

"For what? For being a beautiful precious creature who needs to give her heart before she can give her self? I wouldn't have you any other way."

Mac held her close as tears trickled down her face. He murmured soft words as he stroked her hair. All the time his eyes never lost a glint of their steel. No, he would not have her any other way, but have her he would. Heart, soul and body. There was nothing more certain.

Lessons

❧ ❧

The autumn had given way to winter. Christmas had been and gone. Elen had now become a regular but still not overnight visitor to Mac's flat. But only on weekends. Mac was busy with his work during the week and often worked late into the night. She had got used to his phone being switched off and the late night muffled phone calls telling her how much he loved her. Christmas had been agony – as he had to return to Italy to see Bibi and spend time with his children. She wasn't allowed to call him as he didn't want to spoil his children's Christmas. That was fair enough. It must be hard when your parents are separated. She admired his devotion to his family. He could give her no indication as to how long the divorce would take. He said it was "complicated." Elen was happy though. At every turn he showered her with attention and affection. He had been away visiting Bibi for a few days. She was growing older and hadn't been too well. Just a cold – Bibi had insisted, but Mac was concerned. He would return tomorrow and then he and Elen would spend some quality time together. She could hardly wait.

Elen was distracted today. She couldn't seem to concentrate on anything. She decided to clear out her room. Piles of unsorted through junk had been accumulating for months, and she was rapidly running out of floor. Soon she was happily sorting things into more usable piles and was amazed at how much stuff she could actually throw out. It was cathartic. Throwing rubbish away always made her feel very self righteous. As she pulled out a box from beneath the bed something caught her eye. Elen's gaze fell on the pink wrapped parcel from Rhys. She hardly saw him now. They had studiously avoided each other for the last two months. She had been so cross with him that day that she had never even opened his present. She picked it up and looked at it carefully, trying to catalogue its virtues. It wasn't the best wrapped parcel she had ever seen, but it was a good attempt for a boy. The bow was half wonky and the sticky tape showed. But it had been done with affection and that realisation brought up a curious mix of emotions. She undid the bow, peeled back the sticky tape and took out a book. It was a book of Welsh folk tales, some dating back centuries. She smiled and hugged it to herself. This was a gift that had been chosen with care by someone who knew what was important to her. This would fit in beautifully with the work that she had to do on her project. She flicked through the pages noting the stories. Pwyll and Rhiannon, Branwen – she knew these from her study of the four branches of the Mabinogion. The next one was new to her. "The Dream of Macsen". She picked up the book.

Macsen, the emperor of Rome was a wise man and everyone was very fond of him. He went out hunting with thirty two kings in the woods around Rome. He hunted until midday but became separated from his party. The sun was hot upon his neck and he felt a great desire to sleep. He began to dream. In his dream he journeyed along a valley, following the river to its source high in the mountains. He travelled to the highest mountain in the world, to a land where no man had ever been. At the other side of the mountain he found the most beautiful city and wandering along its harbour, came to bridge made of whale bone. He crossed the bridge and found himself on craft made of gold and silver. He unfurled the sails and sailed away.

After many days and nights, he knew not how many, he came upon an enchanting island, the greenest and richest he had ever seen. He traversed the island and found a huge castle with a large banqueting hall. The ceiling was adorned with gold and coloured gems and ornate paintings covered every wall. He saw two red haired youths playing chess with gold pieces on a silver board. The young men were dressed in satin decorated with precious stones. They wore shoes of the finest leather. Sitting on an ivory throne was a grey haired man. He wore bracelets and a torc of gold. Before the old man sat a girl on rose-gold throne. She wore a white satin gown with a golden mantle. Macsen had never seen such a beauty. She rose from her chair and came towards him. Macsen held her in his arms and as soon as he touched her he found himself once more awake with the sound of his hounds baying in the distance.

Where, Elen wondered, had she heard this story before?

Macsen returned to Rome but his heart was filled with sorrow. No where could he find peace without the girl with whom he had fallen in love. Each time he slept he saw again the beautiful maiden but as soon as his lips touched hers the dream was broken and he found himself alone. He called together all the wise men in Rome. He sent messengers throughout the Empire but after a year no one had found the girl. Macsen became pale and thin. He could find no rest. He sent thirteen men to the place where he had had the original dream and bade them journey as he had done. They did this and they too found the magical ship. They landed on the Isle of the Mighty and there saw the castle and found the youths playing chess and the old man exactly as Macsen had foretold.

They greeted the girl in the rose gold throne "Hail Empress of Rome. What is your name?"

"Do not mock me Sirs. I am Elen Llwydog of Wales" replied the girl

"We do not mock, my lady. We come from Macsen emperor of Rome and he has sent us to ask you to be his wife."

"If that is his desire, then he must ask me himself" replied the girl.

The messengers returned to Rome. Macsen was overjoyed and travelled day and night without taking sleep until he arrived at the Island of the Mighty. He burst open the doors of the castle and took the girl he loved into his arms. As soon as she saw him she fell in love with him and agreed to be his wife.

Macsen stayed in the Island of the Mighty for seven years. Another man was elected to be emperor of Rome and he sent emissaries warning Macsen that should he return or try to take up power again he would be killed. Macsen returned to Rome, conquering Gaul on his way. He slew the new Emperor and he ruled for the rest of his days in peace and prosperity with Elen at his side.

Suddenly Elen felt very cold. She went over the story that Mac had told her about his magical dream. Every detail was etched in her mind. She read over the legend again. No, there were too many similarities. Had he just recited an old legend to her? And she had fallen for it. She felt sick to the pit of her stomach. Her mind flashed back to the things which caused her to feel uncertain. Why, was she never allowed to call him – only the other way round? Was it really to do with work? She knew he was married. Why was there no progress with the divorce? She recalled with pain the paler band of skin on the fourth finger of his left hand. If the marriage was truly over then why did it look as though he still sometimes wore his wedding ring? Was it really just to please Bibi, who he said was too old and frail to cope with the reality of his marriage ending?

Her thoughts flickered to Rhys. Although they had stayed

out of each other's way as much as possible she couldn't forget the hurt look in his eyes every time they had bumped into each other. He was polite – Rhys was always polite. Rhian was still seeing Splodge. Word filtered back to her that Rhys had been neglecting his studies. He was actually thinking of quitting the course and giving up teaching altogether. Elen had tried to talk to him – she knew how much he loved to teach – it all seemed wrong. But there was so much awkwardness between them now that she couldn't broach the subject. She missed the closeness they had. Being with Rhys had always been easy. All she had to be was her self. Now, she felt that she was tying herself in knots trying to become the sophisticated woman Mac deserved at his side. Part of her longed for the simplicity of being with Rhys. She remembered the soft blue of his eyes – his generous smile. The way his eyelashes curled up at the corners. She had made her choice. Decisions have consequences and they can be hard to live with. In that moment she ached for what she had lost.

Her phone rang. It was Mac.

Back into Hiding

❧   ❧

Mac was meeting her for coffee and it wasn't the weekend. Elen had hardly slept wondering about the legend she had read. The more she thought about it the more contrived the whole thing seemed. She made sure that she was as least twenty minutes late as she window shopped along the high fashion shops of Cardiff's castle quarter. He could wait. She was choosing her words carefully – rehearsing the speech in her head. She knew that once she had started she had to keep going. If she allowed Mac's mellow voice to interrupt she would be derailed completely.

The heady aroma of coffee from the expensive bistro spilled into the street, wafting on the breeze to seduce all but the most stoic into its leather clad interior. From the doorway she could see him, anxiously looking at his watch. He looked up and his whole face lit up with a generous smile. Elen could feel her legs turning to jelly once more. She had to fight to get back in control. She had more dignity than this. He met her at the door.

"I was worried. Is everything OK?"

Without waiting for an answer he put his arm around her shoulder and steered her to a table.

"What would you like? They have a wonderful selection. With what can I tempt you?"

His eyes shone with the meaning in the words. With what indeed! The heavy perfume of the coffee drowsed her senses. As he kissed her cheek she breathed in the subtle scent of his aftershave. She struggled to stay on her feet.

"Hot chocolate please, and a piece of the torte"

He beamed.

"The food of the gods for my fairytale princess."

"Well" she thought "I have a few questions to ask about your fairytale."

She watched him walk over to the counter. He was so graceful, like a panther, every move effortless, every sinew straining to show off his well toned physique to its absolute perfection. Elen had never seen a more beautiful man in her life. Well, not in the flesh anyway. Her mind flicked to her favourite film scenes – the bit in "Chocolat" where Roux kisses Vianne, and that spine tingly bit in "Benny and Joon" where Sam strokes Joon's face. She sighed. A beautiful man, aroused, in love but in total control. That was what she wanted – a 'Johnny Depp' look-a-like with the same honesty and integrity. That was what she thought she had recognised in Mac. But was it a lie? She had to find out.

He returned to the table and sat opposite her, sleeves rolled to just below the elbow, his tanned forearms resting against the table with his elegant fingers entwined in front of him. Elen took in the well manicured nails. Her eyes unconsciously traced down the line of the fourth finger of his left hand. The skin still showed a slightly lighter band. It seemed even more heavily defined now than she had remembered it. She felt a cold chill run through her. All the warmth which had bathed her only a few days ago suddenly froze as if hit by a January north wind.

The waiter brought their drinks and her cake. Mac's fingers curled around the edges of his cup of strong black coffee. Elen lunged purposefully at the torte with her cake fork. She raised it to her lips and it melted into soft rich crumbs on her tongue. At any other moment it would have been exquisite, but now, she tasted nothing. All of her senses had shut down.

"I have been doing some reading" she said at last, and as nonchalantly as she could manage. The fork again savaged the torte.

"A beauty who also reads! And why not? A goddess should reach perfection."

His white smile lost none of its charm, but Elen was not convinced. He seemed so different all of a sudden. Shallow. Was that what she was picking up on?

"I have something to show you."

Mac leaned over the table. His head was almost touching hers. He drew his chair in closer. She could feel the warmth of his thigh casually – too casually now– next to hers. She moved away. She reached down and took out Rhys's birthday present to her from her bag. She turned to the carefully marked page and laid the book in front of Mac.

"The Dream of Macsen. Que es? What is it?"

Elen's voice faltered.

"A story. A myth. History. A lie. You decide."

He raised his eyebrows and looked at her. She sat back in her chair saying nothing. Mac took a pair of black rimmed glasses from his jacket pocket and began to read. Half way down the second page he stopped.

"But this! This is my dream!"

Elen held herself down in her chair, her hands gripping the underside of the seat.

"I thought you might recognise it."

Her tone was ice tinged with panic. How much deceit was here? Now she would find out.

"But where? How did you get this? Is it a true history? Who was Macsen? It says he was Emperor of Rome – I don't recall an emperor of that name."

"Well, you seemed to recall everything else didn't you."

Mac stared open mouthed. Elen kept her self control. She told herself to breathe. She went over her bullet-pointed list in her head.

- Find out if he was lying.
- Find out if he's still properly married.
- Find out what his intentions are.

There were more, she was sure there were, but she just couldn't think. She tried to read his face but it was expressionless. Surely that meant that he had made it up. Mac was so clever. Did he really think she wouldn't find out? What was the purpose of such subterfuge? This was the question that had kept her awake most of the night. She had gone over and over it in her head and could only come to one conclusion. Tears began to sting her eyes but she held them back. She stared at Mac, immaculate as always in his designer suit. His hair fell over one eye; he looked boyish despite his age. He was still cool – so very cool. Didn't he care? Elen didn't see how he could. She struggled for the words, then blurted out

"So what was it to be then Mac? A holiday romance? A little fling on the side? Another notch in your hand made leather belt? Another lie – like the ones to your wife?"

Mac's faced twitched momentarily at the last accusation. It told Elen all she needed to know. Inside she was on fire with fury.

"Yes – I had noticed the pale band on your ring finger. That would have been gone long ago if you weren't still wearing your ring."

Mac stood up.

"No! You misunderstand. We are separated. You know this. For months. And this legend – I had no knowledge."

Elen stood up also – hardly caring that they were making a scene.

"You must have thought I was such a fool. Silly little country girl being completely taken in by the big city boy and his romantic tales. Yes, you were right. I did believe you. But I don't believe you now."

Hot tears were streaming down Elen's face. She had promised herself not to cry. She grabbed the book from the table, picked up her bag from the back of the chair and rushed blindly out of the bistro. Salt water stung her eyes and as she turned the corner out of the arcade she felt the cold soft touch of snowflakes against her cheek. She looked up. The clouds were white and full. The snow caressed her eyelashes and soothed the heat on her skin. Her heart beat began to return to normal. She took a deep breath and headed for the car park. She did not want to stay in the city a moment longer than necessary. She had thought she was a butterfly eager to spread her lovely wings – but she wasn't ready. She was too inexperienced. She had been drawn to the subtle beauty of Mac's light and now she had been scorched. Time to hide – to go back to being a caterpillar. But there are some things that you just can't put back.

She consciously took the side streets, keeping out of view just in case Mac was following. She knew he would have to pay in the cafe and that had given her precious moments to escape. She put the coins in the machine, found her car and switched on the engine. Her phone was ringing but she ignored it. The car swung out of the car park and into the street. As she turned into the tree lined avenue she saw Mac standing there, waving frantically. She stared him full in the face and drove on.

Choices

❧ ❦

Why wasn't Rhys answering? Elen put down her mobile phone and fingered the pages of the book he had chosen for her with such affection. She had been unable to get Rhys out of her head since Sunday afternoon.

Ok, Mac was stunning and Rhys wasn't, well, conventionally handsome. He had lovely hair, the most amazing blue eyes which sparkled when he laughed and a broad grin which almost took over the whole of his face. There was something incredibly safe about Rhys. He was big, but not threatening. When she was with him she felt protected. He was sensitive, vulnerable even, but with a very definite manly strength to him. He was one of life's very few gentlemen, she knew she would never have to fight him off and yet, every now and then there was a very real promise of passion in those cornflower blue eyes. In fact, when she thought about it, Rhys was everything she had always wanted in a man – loyal, affectionate – if only he wasn't quite so backwards in coming forwards!

Elen got cross with herself. What was it exactly that she wanted? She got really scared if a bloke came on too strong and would normally run a mile from anyone who seemed too keen. With Rhys she could be herself. It was so easy. It seemed that he could just see into her soul and accepted her for the person she was inside. Wasn't that what she had always said she was looking for? She had felt so alone without him over the past few months. Like a part of her was missing.

So why did she feel this abject frustration that he hadn't impulsively take her in his arms, almost squeezed the life out of her, and kissed her with an intensity that made her head spin? Maybe she should have told him what she wanted. But that would have made her sound like a tart. Maybe she should, God forbid, have made the first move as Rhian kept telling her to. But that might have made him think that more was on offer than she was ready for. What was she ready for? She thought about what she should say to him. How much she had really missed him. But what if he hadn't missed her? And worse – what if he rejected her? Being turned down by any other man would be humiliating – but to lose Rhys completely – that would be like losing her soul.

Why did it have to be so flaming complicated? And why wouldn't he pick up his phone?

Her phone rang again. Mac's name flashed on the tiny phone screen. She pressed the red button to end the call. There was no way that she was going to speak to him now. She felt very very foolish. How could she have been taken in by him?

Rhian rang.

"You ok?"

"Yeah."

"Did you go to see Mr Sex on Legs?"

"Who?"

"Your Italian stud!"

"What? Oh, yeah. I told him to go sling his hook."

"You did what? Why?"

Elen did not want to explain. It was bad enough knowing that she had been taken for a ride, without other people knowing too.

"Na. He was too old. And it was like you said — all that stuff about having seen me in a dream. You know, I mean, come on — a line like that might work over a bottle of red wine and candlelight, but in the cold light of day...."

Elen's voice trailed off.

"Well if you are sure you don't want him you could always give me his phone number!"

Elen could hear the grin on Rhian's face over the phone.

"You would be welcome to him Rhi — but I wouldn't do that to a friend."

"What happened then? You seemed to be all loved up. I thought you were a match made in heaven."

"A match made in fairyland more like."

"What?"

"He was stringing me along Rhi. He's still married — I'm sure of it. And all the stuff about the dream — he got it all out of a book. I found the story. It was pretty much identical."

"What a slime ball. Still he was loaded — in more ways than one. I would have at least had my money's worth before kicking him out of bed."

Elen was aghast.

"Rhian — you don't mean that? Really, you don't, do you?"

Elen wasn't sure of the sincerity of her friend's voice when she said

"Course not. Only joking."

There was a pause.

"So, what's next on the agenda? You going round to pin bag boy to the sofa?"

Elen felt a sharp pang across her chest at the mention of Rhys.

"What? No. I told you, Rhi, he's not interested. He isn't even answering my calls at the moment. We've hardly spoken for the last two months."

"But you still like him though. I've seen the look you get in your eyes when he comes into the room. You never really got him out of your system did you?"

The question was telling.

"That's beside the point. He spent hours and hours with me and never made a move. If he had wanted more than friendship he had plenty of opportunity. Then he goes and cuts me dead because I'm seeing someone. What kind of friendship is that?"

"More fool him then. Els, you can do better than that. You pulled Cardiff's answer to Pierce Brosnan – even if he did turn out to be a slime bag. Bag boy would be well lucky to get off with you."

"Yeah. I guess. Look Rhi, I've just got out of one messy relationship and I don't think it's fair or sensible to go hurtling into another one. But I would like to repair the damage to my friendship with Rhys. That's all it is."

"Ok. If that is what you really think. It's your life. But in my experience the best way to get over a bloke is to go get another one."

"That's you. It's not me."

"As I said – your choice."

Elen sounded resolute but she really felt much less sure about everything. In her heart she was beginning to feel that Rhys was the one for her and that she had made a big mistake. But was it too late to put that mistake right?

The Ice Man

❧   ❧

Mac stood in the snow waving at Elen as her car sped past him. His head felt too light but his heart was sinking. He was only just taking in the possibilities of what Elen had shown him. If the legend was true then did that really mean that it was happening again? That he was its heir and was going to rise to the position of great power that he craved? He went over Bibi's words over and over again in his head. "Listen to your dreams. Beware of a powerful woman." Certainly he had lost his senses over Elen – but was she either dangerous or powerful? Playing around while he was negotiating was a very bad idea. It was something he would not normally do under any circumstances. But she was intoxicating. If this was all part of some master plan suddenly it all made sense.

But she didn't believe him. He could understand why. If he had have been in the same position he would not have believed it either. He had to convince her. He rang her number again. Still no answer. He grimaced. He would have to see her in person. Which presented a problem. Although they had been "dating" for the last few months he had been very careful where to meet her. He had never been to her home. He half guessed, (and in this respect he was correct), that her father would know men who worked at the factory he was trying to take over. He didn't want word of his courting a young woman to become common knowledge. In fact he didn't want it to become knowledge at all. The board of directors at home were all strict Catholics and would take a very dim view of him having an affair with a girl almost young enough to be his daughter. Added to which, his integrity and ability to concentrate on the task in hand would be called into question.

But if Bibi was right – and in his experience she always was – then Elen could be the key to it all. She had always said that his marriage to Kata was wrong. Should he then, set things right by divorcing Kata and marrying Elen? Then, just like in the legend, all of the things he had dreamed of as a child would come true.

He thought back to his childhood. He remembered one holiday – some years after his mother died. He would have been about fourteen years of age. They went to stay with his grandmother's family who were then living on the tiny island of Mallorca. It was a small village, set in the hills. The people worked long hours. Bibi's father was the only one of the family who had tried to settle. Everyone else felt the urge to roam and was stifled trying to live in one place. Mac had stayed there for a summer running barefoot up the winding mountains with its wizened olive groves and ancient fig trees. The village was small. It boasted a church (of course), a taverna and a small café which sold the most wonderful ice creams. Mac watched the local children eating them outside on the pavement with envy. His family had no money, and nothing to trade.

One hot afternoon Mac saw a girl waiting outside the shop. She was plump and plain looking. Her greasy black hair straggled over less than appealing eyes. He would have passed her by, but at that moment the owner of the café came out. He quickly learnt that the girl was the daughter of the owner – and Mac took his chance. He befriended the girl, winning her confidence. Her name was Maria. Mac told her that she was

143

beautiful. At first she did not believe him, but Mac stayed faithful – even enduring the jibes of the other boys. He didn't even seem to care when they public taunted him. Once he even kissed her in front of them. After all, it was only for a summer – Mac knew he would never go back. The rewards were great though. Each day she would bring out huge fantastical concoctions of ice cream, sorbet and sweet fruits. Each day the other boys would watch in envy. And when they were gone Mac enjoyed sweetmeats of another sort. The summer ended and Mac left for Italy. She wrote to him every day for two months. Mac did not write back. He had never intended to.

But that was in the past. He was his own man now and he was determined that he would never be hungry or humiliated again. There had to be a purpose to his dream. Finding out about the legend confirmed it. He would have to convince Elen that he truly loved her. That would mean the risk of a home visit. He would have to be cautious. Time his visit carefully. How could he convince her? Bibi. That was it. He would have to take her to see Bibi.

His thoughts were interrupted. He reversed the car into his parking space. Carla was as efficient as ever when he walked into the office. She handed him a file.

"The stats you wanted."

"How do they look?"

"Which set?"

"The ones we are showing them."

"As you wanted them to. The world trend is downwards. If they take the gamble to go on their own it's not going to be pretty."

Mac beamed at her.

"Good girl."

He clenched the fingers of his left hand around the edge of

the file. He walked back towards his desk then turned as if something had just struck him.

"Carla?"

"Yes?"

"Is your computer connected to the net at the moment?"

Carla mentally raised an eyebrow. What was he up to?

"What would you like me to look up?"

For a split second the immaculate smile vanished from his face.

"No matter. We have got some work to do for this afternoon."

Mac checked the figures for his presentation. He re-jigged the power point pages to best effect. He found it hard to concentrate. He struggled to bring his brain round to the task in hand. Before long he was once again totally absorbed by his task. By 2.30 he was ready. He stood up.

"Right. Showtime."

Carla walked over and straightened his tie. His eyes held her gaze.

"I can't have you going to a meeting less than perfect can I?"

"That's why I employ you, Carla. Your superb eye for detail. And a few other things…"

Mac deliberately ran his eyes over Carla's body. He smiled. Carla couldn't work out if he was sincere or not. But there was little time for speculation. Five minutes later they were driving towards the meeting that could make or break Mac's career.

Burnt Bridges

೪   ೫

Rhys looked at his phone. Another call from Elen. What was she playing at? Had she really thought that Splodge would keep her romantic liaison a secret – and that he wouldn't find out? It had been so hard to face her the next day. He had really tried to keep out of her way but they kept bumping in to one another. It just didn't get any easier. She still had the same effect on him. He couldn't bear the thought of her being with someone else but there wasn't anything he could do about it. And what kind of girl was she anyway – to lead a guy on then go off with the first Flash Harry that appeared on the scene? He had spent three long months trying to get over her. He wasn't going to give in now.

The phone beeped again. A text message this time asking him to pick up the phone and telling him that she needed to see him. Why was that? Probably to officially dump him three months down the line. In anger he texted back.

"I don't think I have anything that I want to say to you at the moment."

The phone rang again. Rhys turned it off.

Then he turned his attention to his college work. He wasn't going to let some girl ruin his future – even if she was everything he wanted. He picked up at book and began to read. It made no sense. He couldn't concentrate. He shut the book and picked up Guinness's lead.

"Come on girl. Do you want to go for a walk?"

The dog bounded with delight at his feet.

Rhys put his phone down on the table and headed for the door.

The Emperor Plans His Campaign

৵ ৶

The meeting had not gone quite as well as Mac had hoped. They had made progress but he hadn't sewn things up. He just didn't seem to have his usual edge.

He and Carla walked to the car in silence. Mac knew that he should be firing on all cylinders, coming up with a dozen permutations to salvage the situation, but all he could think of was how he was going to win Elen back. This was so unlike him. Even in the first heady days of his obsession with Kata he was always in control.

What was it? Was it really this slip of a girl that had him turning somersaults or was it something more? Mac had an uneasy feeling that his destiny was calling him. The legend that he had re-read that morning had unnerved him. Mac would never have admitted it, but he was superstitious. He always carried the saint Christopher his mother had given him on his key ring along with his grandmother's talisman. He wanted to get on the next plane and talk it all over with Bibi. She would know what to make of it. His mind kept going over and over the vision that he had. It had been easy to put it aside until now, telling himself that it had just been the feeble attempts of his fevered brain to make sense of things whilst he was unconscious. Then, when he had seen the castle, his heart had begun to race. Meeting Elen was too much of a co-incidence.

She was just as he remembered her. Was his brain playing tricks on him?

Now, he had more to think about. If his vision was an echo of a real event then what were the implications? Were powers that he could not even begin to comprehend drawing him it to something he could not control? Was he, like Macsen Wledig, destined to rise to a position of great power? And if this was so, was marriage to the lovely Elen the key that would set the whole thing in motion? Mac was beginning to believe that it was. He had to find her and convince her. Everything else fell into second place.

They reached the office. Carla went to the bathroom. Mac turned to her computer. He pulled up multi map and typed in Elen's address. The map appeared on the screen. It made no sense. He zoomed out a little. Now he knew where he was. He printed out the map.

"Did you find what you were looking for?"

Mac had been so intent on his task that he had not noticed Carla return to the office. She was standing behind him now. Normally a sixth sense would have told him he was being observed. He did not know how long she had been there, or if she had seen the map.

"What? Oh, yes. Thanks."

He could not even think of a clever explanation of his actions. He closed down the screen and began to look at something else. The printer chugged to a halt. Carla reached to get the paper but Mac was quicker.

"Thank you. I'll take that."

He put the paper in his top pocket.

Explanations

❧ ❧

Elen sat on the sofa with her laptop in front of her. Beside her was the pile of books she had been meaning to wade through. She wasn't getting anywhere today. She decided to make herself a cup of coffee. She didn't really need one, but it was a distraction and she badly needed something, anything, to take her mind off Rhys and Mac. The doorbell rang. Through the frosted glass she could see a figure at the door. It was hard to make out but the figure was tall. Even before she opened the door she knew who it was.

"What are you doing here?"

Mac looked her straight in the eye. His usual self-assurance had gone completely.

"I had to see you."

"Why?"

"I'm in love with you."

"Really?"

"I haven't actually been in love before."

"But you were – are – married"

"So?"

"People are supposed to be in love when they get married."

"I did suppose I was in love. But it wasn't like this."

"Like what?"

"Like I can't get you out of my head. Like every waking moment is filled with you. Like I'm only half living until I see your face. Like nothing else really matters – not even my all-important high-powered job that I've made the centre of my universe for the last fifteen years. What have you done to me Elen? You've turned my life completely upside down."

Elen stared at him in utter confusion. His whole demeanour had changed. His usual self-assurance was nowhere to be seen. Although he was over fifteen years her senior it was a small frightened boy who stood before her now. The sincerity shone in his eyes. He was completely lost. Instinct took over. She held out her arms and he buried his face in her hair. It felt so good to have the warmth of another human body close to hers. She realised that she was actually very lonely. She wondered if she could dare to believe him.

"But what about your "vision"? Was it just a line? I can't believe you – it's too convenient."

"No, Elen, please believe me. I know it looks really bad but, honestly, I had never heard of the story until you showed it to me. I have no explanation. And that's another thing that has me completely freaked out."

Elen pulled back and looked straight into his eyes. Yes, he was telling the truth. But what other possible explanation could there be? She studied his face. He took her hand and held it close to his cheek.

"Elen, I don't know WHAT to make of your legend. It was spooky enough finding that the castle I had seen in my dreams was real. I managed to convince myself that it had just triggered some childhood memory. I couldn't really believe that I had a real vision. That doesn't happen in the 21st century now does it?"

"I don't know. Part of me always wanted to believe in fairy tales and happy every afters but in reality I don't know if they ever happen. It's an ideal. Something we all wish for. Can wishes come true? It's just so very much easier to believe in things going wrong. At least you know you won't be disappointed."

Mac placed his hands on the sides of her face and tilted it to face his. He looked deep into her eyes.

"Elen, until a few weeks ago I was the world's biggest cynic. I knew the cost of everything and the value of nothing. Nothing really mattered to me that much, not even my family. In some senses they were as replaceable as a new car or the latest must have gadget. I was living my life on automatic pilot. I fooled myself into believing that I came alive when I was negotiating or when the next big bonus came in. I relied upon no one but myself and I wasn't even aware enough of my heart to give it away. How can a man love when nothing ever really moves him? Do you know what they call me?"

She shook her head.

"The ice man. They say that nothing ever melts me, Elen. They were right. I prided myself on that. But now, Elen Lloyd, everything has changed. You have me in the palm of your hand. I am powerless to do anything but to run to you. What do I have to do to win your heart?"

The mantelpiece clock in the living room chimed twelve. Elen looked up. Her father would be home for lunch soon. She needed to talk to Mac alone and couldn't handle her father blustering in with his list of 'essential to be asked' questions. She scribbled a note to say that she had gone out and would see him later.

"Come on. We need to go some place we can really talk."

"Where do you suggest?"

"I don't know. How did you get here?"

"Car."

"Good. Then you can drive."

An Unexpected Development

❧ ❦

They drove across the Rhigos Mountain towards the Beacons. Sheep huddled together against the cold on the slopes. The sky was pale grey and still full of snow. The tops of the mountain had been icing sugar coated. They sparkled under the weak rays of the late winter sun. On the road the snow had already turned to black slush, churned by car wheels and laced with grit and salt. They had lost all of their former glory – like a once lovely woman who suddenly wakes to find that time has stolen the sheen from her skin and blurred the once elegant lines of her curves. Winter washed out the colour from the landscape as the years had washed out the roses from her cheeks. The stark contrasts played up the scars carved by relentless streams – each one highlighted in sharp focus by the grey light. But at least she had the comfort that spring would once again bring the youth back to her face, and for now the higher ground was still stunningly beautiful.

They crossed the mountain down into the valley and then upward once more towards the national park. They passed through the pretty village of Penderyn, still dotted with buildings which went back centuries. The Lamb Inn, once the gaol which housed the scapegoat for the Merthyr Rising and the old farm of Bodwigiad, once family home of the Pritchards and Games families in the sixteenth century. Higher up now, the snow covered landscape dotted with farms which in their way were almost as old as the hills themselves. Life was harsh here, but it had been peopled from almost the first days that man walked on this island. The mountains weaving their own magic to draw the people to them.

Before them lay Pen Y Fan, the highest mountain of the chain. Its peak was lost to the mist. Elen had climbed it when she was a girl, in the sweet days when the only worries were whether or not she would get home in time to watch a favourite program or if so-and-so in school would invite her to their birthday party. In those days, when she was still a child.

She grew up overnight when her mother died. "Children are resilient" people will tell you. Because they may not be able to articulate their loss grown-ups often perceive it to not be there. There was no one that Elen could talk to. Her father was so locked in his grief that to have tried to intrude on it would have been unthinkable. She suddenly had to become mother to him, as well as to herself. There had been plenty to keep her busy, of course. To take her mind off the desperate emptiness which often threatened to engulf her. How could she now love, when the mere action of allowing herself to fall meant the possibility of losing that love again? She had to be very very sure before she could allow that to happen.

They passed the Storey Arms and began the stunning descent into the old market town. Elen spoke only to give Mac directions. He was silent, lost in his thoughts. They drove through the town and up the hill to the boathouse. Mac parked the car facing the river. There were only a couple of other cars in the car park. The air was still crisp and the sky still held the promise of snow. The fields on either side of the river were still white. A family of ducks made their way along the bank and slipped silently into the water. On land they had looked awkward, clumsy. Once in their element they became graceful

154

and serene. Elen knew that their legs were paddling hell for leather under the water. The analogy fitted her perfectly. Inside, her stomach was churning and her heart was pounding, but on the surface she was perfectly still. She wondered how Mac was feeling.

He took her hand and they began to walk along the riverbank away from the town. His fingers curled around hers and stroked her skin reassuringly. The trees were just beginning to put on their first green shoots. Despite the recent snow there was already blossom on the almond trees. As they passed the wind shook the branches and the petals fell down like scented rain over their heads. Mac stopped and turned towards her. The noise of the river fell into a distant hush. The birds stopped singing. Nature was holding its breath.

Then Mac slowly dropped to one knee in front of her. Elen stared in alarm. What on earth was he doing?

"Elen Lloyd."

She looked down at him. His eyes were filled with the most exquisite tenderness.

"What?"

"Will you marry me?"

This was the last thing that she had expected. Her head reeled. Marry him? He must be serious. He must really love her. Could it all really work out? Was he the prince charming that she had always dreamed of? She struggled to find the words in her head. How was she supposed to answer this? No one had ever told her what to say under such circumstances. He looked up at her, still caressing her hand. Elen felt a surge of warmth run through her. Long before her senses were again in check she heard herself saying

"Yes."

Mac put his arms around her and swung her from the ground.

"I love you Elen Lloyd. I. LOVE. YOU."

She heard herself laughing, and his laugh echoing hers. The world was spinning in a haze of palest green. She had just been proposed to. She thought that she should feel light and happy. She smiled. But somewhere deep inside her she still felt like the duck on the water. All was serene on the outside but underneath all was not quite as it should be.

The Sage

❧   ❦

Elen stared out of the plane window. She was going to Italy. For the first time in her life. Beside her sat the man who only yesterday proposed to her. Now she was on her way to meet his grandmother, to get her approval. By nightfall she would be back in Wales. Such whirlwind events were the stuff of films — things that happened to Julia Roberts or Meg Ryan — not to ordinary girls from the Valleys. Yet here she was. Mac stroked her hand and pointed out landmarks. There was a lot of cloud that day, but still the view from the air was spectacular.

The stewardess brought their meal. It was standard airplane fare, bland and tasting of cardboard. But she also brought a small bottle of champagne. Mac smiled as he handed Elen her glass.

"Real champagne?"

Elen was impressed. She had never tasted the real stuff before — the closest she had ever got was Asti Spumante. Mac laughed out loud at her amazement and ruffled her hair.

"Of course it's real champagne. We have something to celebrate!"

The bubbles did something strange to her nose, but the taste was warm and sweet. Before long she was aware that parts of her face were going ever so slightly numb. She told Mac, who laughed and called her an innocent. Elen was not used to alcohol. She was glad that she would have a few hours to sober up before she met Bibi. In truth, the anticipation of the meeting filled her with both excitement and dread. She was well aware that Bibi was the most important person in Mac's life. What would she make of his sudden proposal? What would she think about the age difference? At least taking this step had convinced Elen that Mac's marriage was well and truly over. Surely, he would not be taking her to meet his grandmother if this was not the case.

The plane landed at Verona. They had only hand luggage so it was barely fifteen minutes later when Elen walked out of the airport, blinking in the sunshine. Mac collected the hire car. The road out to the lake was wide and busy with lorries heading out all over the country. She noticed that many of them were Swiss or French. She hadn't realised how close they were to the borders. She dozed. She woke with a jolt to the sound of car horns. They had reached the pretty little town of Garda and they were in a traffic jam. There was only one way into the valley, the road was narrow and looked better suited to donkeys. Minutes later she caught her first glimpse of the lake. It was breathtaking. Elen had not been prepared for its sheer size. It was more like a small inland sea than a lake. Flanked by steep mountains with settlements clinging on to the rock, it was more beautiful than she could ever have imagined. Mac pointed out the pink roof of a monastery. Fishing boats bobbed and swayed on the water. It was truly idyllic.

The road narrowed. Scooters zoomed past at breakneck speed, their riders not even bothering with simple safety, such as helmets. Coaches squeezed past each other on the narrowing road which hugged the lake shore. The houses were close together, front doors right on the road, with their shutters still drawn against the morning sun. Mac turned right up an impossibly steep hill. The road twisted and turned alarmingly.

They passed a pretty church with an impressive shrine to Our Lady.

"This is where I had the accident."

Mac's voice was dry. The skid marks and the hole in the fence were still visible. Elen felt herself go cold at the thought. Mac did not look at her. He kept his eyes firmly on the road. They continued upwards. At times it looked as though the road had petered out completely, then Mac would take a sharp turn into what looked like someone's back yard and pick up the road again. Eventually it became a track and minutes later Mac stopped the car outside an old cottage. The roof was pink. The three storied house had extensions on extensions. It seemed to spill out onto the ground in a haphazard fashion. Mac led her through the gate. There were trees in the garden with strange twisted trunks. They looked completely dead. Mac laughed and told her they were fig trees, and that they were actually very much alive. They came to a small wooden door. Its green paint was faded. The whole house was in need of some attention. Mac knocked softly, then, without waiting for a reply, they went in.

The room was quite dark, as the shutters were still drawn. There was a fire in the hearth and the smell of cooking – herbs and meat. A tiny figure in a long skirt with a shawl around her shoulders greeted them.

"Giovanni. Gio mio, *chajoko chavo.*"

She embraced him. Mac picked her up and swung her around. She laughed. Although she was clearly very old, the laughter was like that of a young girl's. Mac put her down again and she patted her grey curls. Her eyes were bright and clear, ageless.

"Bibi, this is Elen."

Elen stretched out her hand, but Bibi stepped forward and hugged her, kissing her on the cheek. Then she held her at arms length looking at her intently. She nodded and said something in what sounded like Italian but with a very heavy accent. Mac laughed.

"What did she say?" asked Elen as the old lady went out of the room.

"She is going to make the tea."

"Tea?"

"Yes, she is going to read your fortune."

Elen was wide eyed. Her eyes were only just beginning to adjust to the darkness of the room. Although they were in a house, the kitchen had the feel of a gypsy caravan. Everything was brightly coloured, with gleaming pots, drying herbs and hand crocheted blankets strewn everywhere. Every inch of space seemed to be occupied. Bibi returned and indicated to Elen to sit. The tea was hot and sweet. Bibi chatted to Mac in a language which was unintelligible to Elen. She sipped her tea, observing the closeness between grandmother and grandson. Mac looked so much younger. His eyes shone like those of a child. His grandmother stroked his hair, a gesture lost in time. Then she turned to Elen. The tea was finished. She took the cup in her hands, placed the saucer on top and swirled the remains around. She turned the cup over, then, she placed it upright again, looking deeply into its contents. Elen watched the ritual. It seemed so absurd that she had great difficulty in not giggling. But Mac's face was stern.

The old lady looked in silence. Then she said, in broken English.

"You are butterfly, soft, pretty – lovely wings to see in the sunshine. You are free, to fly. That is spirit of butterfly. Man comes, sees pretty wings. He catches butterfly. He pins it to wood. Butterfly is still pretty, but spirit is dead. Is butterfly no more."

Mac handed her his cup but Bibi shook her head.

"Not time" she said.

Their visit was brief. Mac decided that they would not eat at his grandmother's house. They took the road south around the lake to the lovely village of Bardolino. They walked along the harbour watching the swans on the lake. The ferry was coming in to dock, creating a wave which swept in to the shore. They walked along the paved lake shore until the road came to an end. Mac turned and led her into a hotel garden.

"We will have lunch here. It's an old favourite of mine."
They sat at one of the tables in the garden. The flowers were just beginning to bud and there was a hint of spring in the air. The head waiter appeared and handed them the menu. Elen was unsure what to order. The waiter smiled.

"Ah, you are not sure what you like?"
Elen nodded. The tall slim man with the immaculately slicked back hair beamed back at her.

"You like spicey?"
Elen smiled. Yes, she did.

"Then for you we make spaghetti cooked with oil of olive, hot peppers, garlic – and love."
Elen blushed. How could she refuse?

"That would be lovely. Thank you."
He nodded.

"And for you, sir?"
Mac looked up.

"I think I will have the same."

"Do you like the wine, Sir?"

"Yes, a bottle of muscato, I think."

"Sweet?"

"Yes. And a bottle of water – frizzante."

The waiter hurried off. Elen looked across the lake at the imposing mountains. This was truly God's chosen spot. The lake had it all, beautiful clear water, birds, fish, mountains, and a mild climate. What more could anyone ask for.

A girl brought the placemats, cutlery and the wine. She poured some for Mac who tasted it and nodded. Then she poured a glass for Elen. It was sweet and potent.

The waiter returned with the spaghetti. Elen looked at the fork, knife and spoon in front of her. How exactly were you supposed to eat it? This was one of the reasons she had always avoided spaghetti in restaurants! The waiter winked at her.

"If you use the knife, I charge you an extra ten pounds!"

She laughed. She could stay here forever. She could imagine herself living here, by the lake. Maybe she could teach at one of the local schools. Surely it wouldn't be too hard to train to teach English as a foreign language. She watched Mac twist some spaghetti around his fork, pushing it against the spoon as he did so. She mimicked his actions. To her surprise it worked and the spaghetti reached her mouth without landing in her lap. It was the most amazing thing she had ever eaten. The spices excited her palette. She looked across at Mac.

"This is wonderful. I've never eaten anything like it."

"Sometimes simple things can be the best."

Elen was totally happy. She looked into Mac's eyes and saw them shine back at her.

But they had to go home. In less than an hour they were on their way back to the airport. Suddenly, Elen felt drained.

"What did she say, your grandmother?"

Mac was subdued.

"She likes you. She thinks you are very pretty."

This was true. Mac was careful not to tell her the other things she had said.

"This is not good, Gio. Finish one thing before you start another, otherwise very bad things will happen."

Mac had told her about the legend.

"Yes, I know it. Magnus Maximus. He was your ancestor.

162

But legends should not always be believed *chajoko chavo*. The truth, that is what is important."

But Mac had not been listening. All he had heard was that Macsen was his ancestor. That told him all he wanted to know.

Tracking

❧ ❧

Carla pressed the button marked "history" on her PC. What was wrong with Mac she thought? She browsed through the internet pages that had been looked at that week. Most of them were hers. What had Mac been looking at that he hadn't wanted her to see? She found the multi-map page and brought it up again on the computer. It gave an address in the Rhondda. They had no dealings there. None of the executives they had been dealing with lived there. What was Mac up to? Could he be double dealing? Certainly he had not performed as he usually did in their last meeting.

Carla decided that she needed to find out more. She dialled Mac's number. It rang but he didn't answer. Carla was not about to let Mac ruin things. She was well aware that in her field a woman had to be twice as good as a man in order to get noticed and this was her golden opportunity. She had gone out of her way to help Mac get this promotion because she knew that he would take her with him. If he fouled up then her chance would be lost. And she was not going to let that happen.

She grabbed her keys and headed for her car. She drove to the apartment the company was renting. Mac's car was not outside. She took the lift to the fourth floor and rang the doorbell. No answer. Then she quietly let herself in. The flat was silent. The living room looked pristine. She walked through to the kitchen. The last traces of breakfast still hung in the air. The smell of strong coffee. Only one cup though. So he had not been entertaining. She checked the bathroom. Only one toothbrush. If he had been seeing another woman she must be very meticulous. Finally she steeled herself to walk into the bedroom. The bed was unmade but relatively tidy. If Mac had tumbled a girl in there the sheets would be on the floor and the pillows would be anywhere but the head of the bed. Yes, Carla knew that. From personal experience.

She stood at the window looking out towards the road. A red car swung into the car park. It was Mac. She watched him park the car and then walk round to the passenger side to open the door for someone. A petite brunette. Young, she noticed. Very young. Mac took her in his arms and kissed her very tenderly. Carla remembered how that felt. She watched him take her by the hand and lead her towards the apartment block. Then Carla picked up her keys, closed the door and left by the stairs.

News

  ⮞ ⮜

Rhian was more than a little drunk. Again.

Splodge and Rhys struggled to keep her upright as they attempted to walk her home.

"The world won't stay still" she complained.

"How much has she had?"

Rhys was not particularly amused. He hated playing gooseberry, but Splodge had insisted that he should go out to take his mind off 'things'. Rhian had reacted to his presence by sulking. As she had less to say she had more time to drink. And drink she did.

From somewhere in her handbag came a dreadful polyphonic ring tone. Rhys attempted to keep her vertical whilst Splodge rummaged in the bag for her phone.

"Elss... My best friend. It's Els. Say hello to my best friend."

Rhian switched the phone to speaker.

"Rhi, you'll never guess what? Mac asked me to marry him."

Rhys felt the colour drain from his face. If there was anywhere else in the world that he could be at that moment that was where he wished himself.

"Ooooh. What did you say?"

It seemed to take forever for her to reply. Rhys clenched his fists.

"I said yes. Rhi, are you there? I said yes!"

Rhys ground his teeth in an effort to stop his eyes from stinging. Splodge took the phone from Rhian's hand and switched it back to normal.

"Congratulations Elen. This is Simon here. Rhi has had a bit too much to drink. We are getting her home at the moment. I'll get her to ring you in the morning."

He put the phone back in the bag and looked at Rhys.

"You ok?"

Rhys stared into space, not trusting himself to reply. The news seemed to have sobered Rhian up a bit. They turned into the street where she lived.

"Can you manage her on your own from here mate?"

"No probs. I think I will probably stay the night. Make sure she is ok. You know."

Rhys nodded. He knew exactly what Splodge meant. He turned away, closing his eyes and breathing hard.

"Damn you Elen Lloyd. I wish I had never met you. I wish..."

The night air whipped at his face, stinging as it mingled with the bitter tears he could no longer hold back.

An Old Ally

℞ ℟

Mac was in the office well before Carla got there. He was bright and breezy and making coffee. He had already reworked the figures for the next meeting and found out some "interesting facts" on their rival bidders by the time she arrived.

He placed a set of files and a cup of coffee on her desk.

"I have some calls to make Carla. I would appreciate not being disturbed for the next half hour or so."

He closed the door on the temporary office they had rented. Carla could see him lifting the telephone receiver and turning his chair away from her. Gently she lifted the receiver.

"Amanda. How are you? It's Mac."

"What do you want?" the woman's voice was very cold.

"Oh, is that any way to speak to an old friend?"

"Is that what you are?"

"Well, an old lover, then."

"Get on with it, Mac. You wouldn't contact me unless you wanted something. Now what is it?"

"You offered Kata some work a while ago."

"And she made it clear you wouldn't allow it. You are still in the Stone Age, Mac. I don't know why she ever married you."

"Ah come now, you do, don't you."

"What do you want?"

168

"Offer her the work again."

"Why?"

"I think it would do her good. She's getting bored being at home all day while the boys are at school."

Amanda laughed.

"And since when did you care for your wife's welfare?"

"Amanda, that is so cutting."

"But true. And why should I do this for you Mac?"

"You know why."

There was a pause.

"There's a name for people like you, Mac."

"Really?"

"But I'm too much of a lady to use it."

"That's something you have never been. Just do it."

Mac put down the phone. Carla carefully replaced the receiver. So, Mac was trying to get Kata to go back to work. Why? She knew he was dead set against it. What was he playing at?

Showtime

❧ ❧

Mac walked into the meeting with a new air of confidence. His hair was gelled within an inch of its life and his suit was immaculate. He drummed the side of his leather briefcase with well groomed finger nails. His dark eyes flicked around the room taking in every detail, every expression. He knew exactly how he was going to play this.

"Gentlemen"

An elderly man got to his feet.

"Mr Maconi, we cannot start yet, Mr Fisher has yet to arrive."

"We did agree on 2.30 Mr Ellis." Mac was curt, but with a smile.

"It is only 2.35, Mr Maconi."

"The telecoms industry does not wait, Mr Ellis, and in any case there are reasons why Mr Fisher is intending to be late, and those reasons do not have anything to do with the welfare of your company."

Another grey suit got to his feet.

"I think you had better explain yourself, Sir. If you are casting doubt on Mr Fisher's integrity...."

At this point the company chairman waved him down. He looked weary. His eyes had lost almost all of their brightness. And with good reason. Just half an hour ago he had a nasty shock.

"Gentlemen. I have an announcement. Earlier today Mr Maconi brought certain facts to my notice. Facts which I believe must make Bowen Electronics reconsider any plans we had to go with BetaCom International's bid."

The room suddenly hushed. The old man looked very frail.

"Would you like me to elaborate?" Mac asked in a voice laced with concern and kindness.

"No, thank you, Mr Maconi. I was personally responsible for employing Mr Fisher. It falls to me to admit that was a mistake."

All eyes were on the chairman. He held on to the table in front of him as he spoke.

"It would appear that we have been deceived. Mr Fisher has, for some months now, been in the pay of BetaCom International. The reports that he has presented to us did not give a clear picture. The truth of the matter is that should we accept their offer, they have every intention of closing us down in a matter of weeks and selling off the site. They already have a buyer. It would appear that at no time did they intend to take on our company as a going concern."

Mac stood back and took in the shocked faces. Then he poured a glass of water from the crystal jug on the table and carefully took it over to the old man. The sad blue eyes met Mac's cold dark steel gaze.

"I am aware that many of you" here Mac nodded towards Ellis and the other grey suits, "do not like the deal with S-Systems. You are worried about the security of your workers."

He paused. He leaned forward, gripping the edge of the long mahogany table.

"Why do you think I do the job I do?"

Silence. If any of them had an opinion there was not one brave enough to venture it now.

"It is because I do not like to see men lose their jobs."

He stood up, to his full height.

"I am acutely aware that every job lost is another family shunted into misery. A misery that my own family lived and breathed when I was a boy."

He looked to the floor, allowing his words to sink in. Then, he lifted his gaze and met their eyes.

"Gentlemen, there are no guarantees in the telecoms business. You know that as well as I do. It is a cut throat market and each of us has to fight for our own survival. But I am here to offer you a lifeline. We will keep the company going for as long as is economically viable. I believe that with the new technology that you have developed, and the financial clout of S-Systems, the situation can be turned around."

They grey suits shifted uncomfortably in their seats.

"Thank you Mr Maconi. I must ask you to leave now whilst the directors discuss your offer."

Mac nodded and picked up his briefcase.

"Thank you gentlemen. I hope you make the right decision."

He gave them a half smile that could have been sincerity or self satisfaction. As the door closed behind him the smile broke into a smirk. He clenched his fist around the edge of the briefcase.

"Gotcha"

Carla was waiting by the car.

"How did it go?"

"All to plan. Whatever you paid that private detective was well worth the money. It was like taking candy from a baby."

"They signed?"

"They will. I would give them an hour tops. And Fisher is for the high jump. The old man was nearly in tears."

She nodded.

"I'll need you to authorise the cheque for the PI."

Mac smiled.

"Pass it over."

Mac did not even query the amount as he signed. Carla eyed him carefully. His dark hair strayed over his slate black eyes. He was still a very attractive man. The suit fitted to perfection, showing off the well toned torso to best advantage. It hugged the broad shoulders and tapered, drawing her eye to his waist, and beyond. Even now, with all that she knew, Carla had to fight with herself not to weaken.

Mac passed the cheque back to her. She stifled a sigh of relief but Mac was gloating too much to notice. His phone rang. He lifted it to his ear.

"Maconi"

He broke out into a broad grin and gave a thumbs up sign to Carla. She smiled. So, the deal was done.

He put down the phone.

"I have to go back up there to tie up the lose ends."

"Ok. I will go back to head office to secure everything at our end."

"Well done, little Carla."

He pulled her close and kissed her full on the mouth. She momentarily pulled away, then succumbed.

"You are completely untrustworthy, Mac Maconi."

He smiled.

"That's part of my charm."

"One day your charm will desert you, Mac. And then, what will you do?"

Mac shook his head.

"Stay one step in front of the opposition until it comes back."

He turned on his heels and went back into the tall grey building. He was on a roll. The deal was sewn up, he had heard from Amanda that morning that Kata had accepted the modelling work that she had agreed in their prenuptial documents never to do again. It was grounds enough for divorce with no blame laid at his door. He would soon have the way cleared to marry the lovely Elen and take his rightful place in the position of great power waiting for him. It was only right, he reasoned. It was his inheritance.

Carla sat in the car and pulled a manila envelope from the glove compartment. She opened it and studied the photograph. Mac and a young girl outside a high class jewellers. She looked at the close up. That ring must have cost him a month's wages. She flicked through the file. At least she had a name now, "Elen Lloyd, age 21, address..." The details stung and she breathed hard to get though them. She turned to the next page. Her brows furrowed with bewilderment. What was this? "The history of Magnus Maximus – known as Macsen Wledig". She put the papers back in the envelope. She would read them on the plane. She certainly did have a lot to attend to when she got back to Milan.

The Promise

୶ ୶

Elen looked across the candle lit table into the eyes of her fiancé. He was glowing. Every part of his being seemed to shine as if his very soul was gleaming before her. She should be so happy. She searched his face as he poured her a glass of champagne. There was no hint of deceit, he really did seem genuinely happy. So why did she have this nagging feeling that all was not well. Were the doubts all her own, she wondered. This had all happened so fast. He stroked her cheek.

"You are so very lovely, my fairytale princess."

She smiled back at him. Was that what he wanted? A fairytale princess? The feelings of unease rose within her.

"Mac?"

"Yes?" he looked quizzical. He took her hand in his. She felt very small, very vulnerable beside him.

"I'm not a princess. I'm just an ordinary girl."

"You are a princess to me. You stepped straight out of my vision and stole my heart. You can't take it back now you know."

"But, we aren't in a fairy tale Mac. This is real life. You would tell me if there was a problem, wouldn't you?"

"Of course. But there is none. The business is going well, I shall have a big promotion soon and in the summer, when my divorce comes through, we shall get married."

"Where are we going to live?"

"We shall have a house here and something in Italy I think. It doesn't matter. As long as I am with the woman I love everything else will turn out wonderfully. Just like in the legend. We have no need to worry, you and I. Our paths have been set since before we were born. All we have to do is to play our parts and be happy. Everything else is decided."

He seemed completely sincere in his belief. Elen looked at him half afraid. He was such a clever man, so in control, so knowledgeable. Surely he knew what he was talking about. If he could have faith then so should she. He kissed her hand, then leaned over the table and kissed her softly on the lips.

"My wonderful dream come true. How much I love you, Elen Lloyd."

His phone rang. Mac put his hand in his pocket to answer it then stopped himself, looking at Elen as if for permission. She smiled.

"It's ok. They can borrow you for a few minutes."

Mac beamed at her and took the small silver object out of his jacket.

"Maconi"

He listened intently.

"Right. Understood."

He nodded.

"I'll be on the first flight out tomorrow."

He closed the flap on the phone and looked at Elen.

"This is it."

"This is what? What has happened?"

Mac lifted Elen to her feet and swung her round.

"You and your magical legend, Elen Lloyd. It's all coming true."

He set her down again and she stared up at him with more than a tinge of fear in her eyes.

"You said you were flying tomorrow. Mac, what's going on?"

"Head office want me to fly back to 'discuss a few matters'"

He seemed completely delighted. Elen was less sure.

"What does that mean?"

"What else can it mean? The deal is signed, sealed and pretty much delivered. They have seen what I can do. They want to discuss a promotion."

"Are you sure? Is that what they said?"

Mac grinned.

"They didn't have to. Giorgio, old fox trying to make me sweat. It's happening, Elen. All that I have ever wanted is all going to be mine."

Elen stared at his face. His features had all gone hard. Even his eyes which used to dance with amusement had turned to stone. She suddenly felt a shiver, as if someone had walked over her grave.

"How long will you be away?"

Mac was at his most animated now. His hand movements had become larger and more elaborated. This was a side of him that Elen had not seen until now.

"I'm not sure. Not more than a few days, I wouldn't think."

Rhian

❧ ❧

The few days had turned into a week. Elen had hardly heard from Mac, and when he did phone his calls were short and he seemed very distant. There were "things that he had to sort out" he told her. She did her best to keep busy. Her thoughts had been so much of Mac just lately that she had neglected her course work. Now, she threw herself into it with gusto. She longed for a distraction though, and it turned up on cue, in the form of Rhian.

Elen could see her friend's familiar shape through the rippled glass of the front door. As she opened the door Rhian spilled in, all bags and giggles.

"Ells – you will never guess what? Never in a million years!"

Elen moved out of the way as the human rhino dragged her luggage through the hall and into the front room.

"You've been shopping?" queried Elen, although the bags were a bit of a give-away.

"What? Yes, of course, it's Saturday, but no, that's not it. It's *why* I've been shopping that's the thing."

Elen looked at the bags for clues. Then came the surprise. Usually when Rhian went shopping she came home with shoes, clothes and make-up. These bags were all from "lifestyle" shops. There were cushions, a throw, a lamp, candles and even a duvet.

"You're re-decorating?" she asked.

"Kind of. I'm moving in with Simon! He asked me yesterday. Isn't it brilliant?"

Elen wasn't sure if congratulations were in order or not. She decided that even if they weren't she would venture them anyway.

"Great. Congratulations. Where are you going to live?"

Rhian carried out pulling purchases from bags. She really had spent a fortune. Elen wondered if Splodge had actually *seen* the vibrant pink fluffy cushions and matching fur throw, (which, incidentally Rhian had *had* to buy as it so perfectly matched the love cuffs he got her for their two month anniversary. Now who says romance is dead?)

"Simon has got us a flat. It used to be his grandmothers, but she went into a home, so he's taken it over. The rent is all paid until august and by then we shall both have jobs. Isn't it brilliant Elen? I'm so excited."

She clearly was. Elen couldn't help but feel happy for her. Who would have thought it, Rhian the queen of the one night stands and Simon P Lodge about to set up home?

"He's over there painting. I'm going over later. We're going to have a house warming party next Saturday. Will you make those cheesy things you do? And the smoked salmon things with the white stuff?"

Elen nodded and laughed.

"Whatever makes you happy."

Rhian dragged Elen to her feet.

"Come and see it with me. Come over and have a look, tell me what you think."

"Rhi – I'm half way through an essay"

Resistance to Rhian was useless. Ten minutes later the back seat of Elen's car was crammed with Rhian's household goods and they were on their way over the Rhigos Mountain. Spring was now well underway. Baby lambs huddled next to their mothers or gambolled excitedly with wiggling tails. The pale green of the new grass contrasted with the deep green of the pines. They passed the stone clearer's hut with its well tended garden of paper flowers and began the descent into the next valley.

As they sped through the village of Hirwaun Rhian said

"Can we stop at a chippie for something to eat? I'm starving."

Elen was getting hungry too.

"Sure thing – no problem."

"I'll ring Si and see what he wants."

Rhian disappeared into the chip shop and returned with a large steaming bag which she placed on her lap.

"Great. Turn left by here. Now right. Up the hill past the college. Now right into the estate. Now right again. Left up here. Here we are. You can park in front of the gate behind the blue car.

The blue car. Elen's heart sank. She recognised that car. Rhys. Oh gawd, what was she going to do now? She momentarily thought about just dropping Rhian off and coming back for her later, but that would appear churlish. No, she couldn't do that. Best to bite the bullet and get it over with.

She helped Rhian in with the bags. The flat was small and still smelt of old person. She took the bags into the bedroom as indicated by Rhian. She could hear the boys' voices in the kitchen. She followed Rhian in. The conversation stopped abruptly.

Rhian was totally oblivious. She pulled out plates from bags, washed them and emptied the pies and chips onto them. Splodge recovered himself and produced brown sauce from the cupboard. Elen found that her heart was pounding. He stood there in an old T shirt and mis-fitting jeans, with paint in his hair. And he looked – wonderful. Why did the sight of him still do that to her? He was so big – he seemed to fill the room with his presence so much so that there was barely air left for Elen to breathe. He stared at her. His mouth half decided between a smile and a pout. He checked himself and found some stools from under the dust sheet. They sat down to eat.

"How are you?"

Elen asked the question without looking at Rhys. She couldn't look. If she stared into those pale blue eyes once more she would be captivated. He was just a man – she told herself. Oh, if only that were true.

"Good. You?"

She knew he was looking at her from under those long eye lashes.

"Doing ok. Almost finished the course work."

"I've done mine. Working on final paper now."

She still didn't look up.

"Oh, I almost forgot. Si – open the fridge and get the bubbly out."

The tension lifted for a second. Both Elen and Rhys visibly relaxed. They watched with amusement as Splodge did as he was told. Elen couldn't believe how well trained Rhian had got him. He poured it into four tea cups and handed them out.

"Here we go then. To our new home."

They raised their cups.

"To Splodge and Rhian and their new kitchen. Long may they cook in her."

Rhian looked at her friend in alarm.

"No fear of that. Not when there's a good chip shop, a choice of three indians and two chinese take aways down the road."

"Long may you eat in it then." Rhys was smiling, all be it briefly.

They clinked cups and drank down the champagne. Elen didn't normally drink much. The bubbles exploded on her tongue and went up her nose. The taste was sweet and potent. She felt the warmth as it went down her throat.

"Where's lover boy then?"

Rhys had to ask.

"He's gone back to Italy."

Rhys looked up, surprised. Their eyes met. Elen had almost forgotten how lovely his eyes were. Cornflower blue with eyelashes that curled up at the corners. And he really did have the most brilliant smile. She felt her knees weaken. It must be the champagne, she reasoned, hoping desperately that it wasn't anything else.

Rhys held her gaze.

"When is he back?"

"I don't know."

Rhys really brightened now. Suddenly he was back to his old self, talking animatedly, telling Elen about his project and the research he was doing with his classes. Elen found him so easy to talk to. The old feelings were surfacing, but so subtly that she was hardly aware of them until it was too late.

His phone rang.

"Mam – no I've had lunch. No, sorry I had completely forgotten. I'll get it now. Ok, fine. Be there in a bit."

He shook his head.

"Sorry, I'm going to have to shoot off. Mam asked me to pick up a chicken from the butcher in town. It completely slipped my mind. I've got to go pick it up."

Splodge got to his feet.

"Ok mate. No problem."

Rhys started to walk out of the door when Elen spotted his coat on the sofa. She picked it up without thinking and started after him.

"Your coat."

He had just reached the front door.

"What? Oh, thanks."

He turned to face her.

"It was good to see you Elen."

Why did she feel so tingly? It must be the alcohol. She would have to sober up before she drove home. Then it happened. Somehow they both leaned in towards each other and the next second they were kissing. His mouth was warm and soft and tasted of champagne. She pulled away. He smiled and waved as he ran down the path with more than a hint of a skip in his step.

Elen closed the door and leaned on it heavily. Oh my God. What had she done?

Home Truths

꙰

Mac put his keys down on the kitchen table. It felt surprisingly good to be home. Kata was out. That suited him. He was tired, and didn't want any complicated conversations. He took a shower and changed his clothes. He chose carefully. He wanted just the right amount of understated professionalism when he accepted his new post.

He picked out the pale orange silk tie. Too flash? No, just right. He has flair; he wanted to show them that. He rehearsed the lines in his head. First to the board.

"Gentlemen, thank you for your confidence in me..."

Did that sound too self-effacing? He shrugged. He couldn't decide what to say. He would think on his feet. That would be more of a challenge.

Then to Kata.

"I can't believe you took on this job, knowing full well how I feel about it. You know I have been offered promotion – high promotion. How is this going to look? Kata, you leave me no choice.."

He smiled to himself. Yes, everything was working out perfectly.

As he fastened his cufflinks he noticed a file on the dressing table. It has Kata's name on it. He opened it without hesitation. It contained her new portfolio. Mac flicked through the photographs. She looked good. Yes, she still looked really good. Well, he thought – he didn't have to end things with her straight away. He could give it a couple of days. He straightened his tie, flicked his jacket over his left shoulder and headed for the door.

The Milan heat hit him as he stepped out of the car. It was a relief to reach the air conditioned building. He went straight to Giorgio's office. He walked in, without knocking.

"Mac, you are back."

"Evidently."

Giorgio never seemed to quite manage style. His shoes were just the wrong shade for his suit. How did he get to be an executive, Mac wondered?

"There are some things that we need to go over before tomorrow's meeting of the board."

Mac leaned back on the leather chair.

"Sure. What things?"

"You indicated to the Welsh directors that we would keep the factory going?"

Mac looked serious.

"I said there were no guarantees. There is nothing in writing. If we can't do that and the site has to close in two months time that is just market forces. Nothing that could be done about it. It was never our intention to strip it and close it down – but, as I told them.."

His eyes gleamed as he relished the remembered moment.

"I'm in the business of saving jobs. Mine. And those at S-Systems."

Giorgio sighed. "Well worded. Ok. Fine. Let's go over the fine details. I don't expect any problems."

Mac nodded. He paused just long enough before saying

"This meeting tomorrow. You said it was an extraordinary meeting of the board?"

Giorgio was tight lipped.

"That's right."

"Why, exactly?"

"You know the type of thing. I'm not going to go into detail Mac."

Mac looked across at him and smiled.

"Promotions, dismissals, new directors etc…"

Giorgio looked him full in the eye.

"That sort of thing."

Mac laughed.

"Ok, Giorgio. Be mysterious if you must. I think I know what is going on. I'll allow you your moment of triumph."

Giorgio stared at him blankly for a second. Then they both got back to their work.

The Mirror Cracks

Elen read the text from Rhys for the third time.

"Glad we got things sorted out – finally. Ring me when you're free. Rhys xx"

She had given him totally the wrong idea. What was she going to do? She had to put things right. She looked at the clock on the mantel piece. It was getting late. She couldn't face talking to him. But a text would seem so cold. She put down the phone and went into the kitchen to make a cup of coffee.

Then she changed her mind. She owed him at least to talk to him.

The number rang. And rang. Then the answerphone.

"Hi, this is Rhys. I can't take your call right now, but if you leave a message I'll get straight back to you."

She sighed. Oh, well. Nothing for it.

"Rhys. It's Elen. I'm sorry if I misled you this afternoon. I don't know how it happened. It can't happen again. Sorry. Take care."

Her voice trailed off as she pressed the end call button. No, she decided. She couldn't just leave it at that. It was cruel. She didn't want to think why she had kissed him that afternoon. Maybe it was the champagne. What if it wasn't the champagne? What if she really still had feelings for him? But she was supposed to be marrying Mac. Mac. Where was he? Why hadn't he called? If he had been there this would never have happened.

She tried to ring Rhys again. Still no reply. She tried to remember where he was going that evening. That was it – a pub quiz. Maybe she should go over. She looked again at the clock. 10pm. No, it was too late – and anyway she had no idea which pub they were going to. If only she hadn't left that message. Now she had made things between them even worse. She didn't want things to be like this. She missed him. Did she? Yes, she did miss him. Did she miss Mac? She wasn't sure.

She lay thinking on her bed for what seemed like hours and finally drifted into fitful sleep. When she awoke it was after midnight. She had to speak to Mac. She just had to.

She rang his mobile number. She felt a sense of relief as she heard it ring. Now she would feel better. She would hear his voice and all would be right with the world again.

"Hello"

Elen went cold.

That was not Mac's voice. Elen instantly realised who she was talking to.

"Kata?"

"Yes, this is Kata Maconi."

Then in the background she heard Mac's voice.

"What is it darling? Leave it. Come back to bed.."

Truth

❧   ❦

Elen ended the call and sat up on the bed. Kata. Kata Maconi. The wife he was estranged from, for months. The woman he was divorcing to marry Elen. She thought of all the things he had said to her. Her mind flashed back to all the times he had talked about their marriage. Always with a reference to the promotion he was going to get which went along with it. Always just as it was supposed to be in the legend. In his dream.

It was a sham. The whole thing was a sham. She should be upset. She should be devastated. But she wasn't. She didn't even feel numb. She just felt – relieved.

Rhys. She had to phone Rhys. She had to undo the damage she might have done with her phone message. She tried his number. It was switched off. She tried again. No luck. She sent a text.

"Rhys. I got it wrong. I've got to see you. Elen x"

Suddenly she realised that she was very very tired. There was nothing more she could do that night. She would see Rhys in the morning. And as for Mac, she didn't give him a second thought.

Preparation

Mac admired his wife's curves as she brushed her long blonde hair. She was a difficult addiction to give up. But he had more important concerns. She was just a pleasant distraction. It would make it easier to be indignant later when she came clean about the modelling job. For now it suited him to ignore it.

"You look the part. All ready for your big meeting."

Mac was surprised. He hadn't mentioned it to her.

"Who told you about that?"

She smiled and touched her nose.

"Carla. We met in town yesterday. She is a very pleasant girl"

Mac was slightly concerned. Then he thought, no, Carla knew the score. She wanted promotion as much as he did. She would do nothing to jeopardise things for him. It would not be in her interest.

Kata fiddled with her ear rings.

"We are having lunch together as a matter of fact."

"Really?"

This was a surprise. Carla must be planning to become his wife's best friend in order to secure her position. Pity she had backed the wrong horse, but then, she wasn't to know that. He had been very careful.

"What time is your meeting with the board?"

"Two thirty."

Kata raised an eyebrow. That was late for a business meeting.

"Not a long meeting then."

"I shouldn't think so."

Kata busied herself getting the children off to school. Mac collected his laptop and briefcase and headed for the door.

"Good luck."

He waved as he got into his car. Here it was. His day had come at last.

Realisation

꒰ ꒱

Rhys wasn't answering his phone. Again. Elen had to see him. She knew now why she had kissed him. This business with Mac had just been a flight of fancy. She had been caught up with all the glamour and romance of it all. It wasn't real. Now she had a grip on reality again and she knew what she wanted. Rhys Harris wasn't going to know what hit him.

Her thoughts went back to the time they had spent together. The way he could look into her eyes and it felt as if he was looking straight into her soul. And that was ok. It was safe. There was nothing in Rhys that could hurt her. Those cornflower blue eyes. The way they sparkled and his whole face lit up when he smiled. The way his shoulders shook when he laughed. The way he took charge without actually being bossy. The way that she just knew everything was alright when she was with him.

What was this feeling? It wasn't something she had felt with Mac. She remembered that kiss. So soft, so gentle. Was she in love with Rhys? She really did think that it was a distinct possibility. That was so scary. She had hated not being with him. Even when she was with Mac he had never been far from her thoughts. But truly being in love? What did that mean? It meant putting yourself at risk of being hurt. But also, maybe, putting yourself at risk of being happy. Was it possible to be really truly happy? She did believe that she could be happy with Rhys. Yes, she knew she could be. Did she deserve to be happy? She didn't know, but she wanted to take the chance. Strange how taking a chance on happiness was far more terrifying than taking a chance on unhappiness.

His phone was still off. She would go round to see him. She had the address on a piece of paper in her purse. She pulled it out and checked the internet for directions. Ok. She had it now. Look out Rhys Harris, I'm on my way.

Carla's Little Meeting

⮞ ⮜

Kata stared at the photographs before her. She said nothing. She could not take her eyes off the face in the photograph, kissing the pretty young girl. Her husband. Her philandering cheating husband.

Carla stroked the back of her hand.

"I'm sorry to have to do this Kata. I just thought that you really ought to know."

Kata was stony faced.

"How old is she?"

"Twenty one I think. Still in college."

Kata felt sick. But she had to ask.

"And you say that he was – is planning to marry this, this little tart."

Carla looked away.

"Yes, he had asked her to marry him. Here they are outside the jewellers. You can see the ring."

Kata closed her eyes. The room was spinning. Last night he had been so loving. So passionate. She thought that things were getting back to the way they used to be. She thought he loved her. Yet, all the time he was planning to leave her and have his way with a girl almost young enough to be his daughter.

"How was he planning to do this? Was he just going to tell me and then let me sue for adultery?"

Carla looked into the hurt tearful Scandinavian eyes. The poor woman. She actually loved Mac. Probably the only person who ever really had, or ever really would. She didn't deserve this. But Mac did.

"He was being far more cunning than that."

Kata was puzzled. Carla took out another file.

"He was blackmailing your agent. He was going to use your work as grounds for divorce. You remember your pre-nuptial agreement?"

Kata nodded.

"I didn't think anything of it at the time. That I should give up modelling. I was expecting Vitto. All I wanted was to be a wife and mother. I didn't really believe he would hold me to it. Carla, how could he be so cruel?"

Carla didn't have an answer. She noticed that Kata didn't even ask what hold Mac had over Amanda. Had she worked it out? Carla had. Amanda's dark eyed daughter, two years older than Vitto. Born just at the time that Amanda's rich husband was setting her up in business. A business that made Amanda one of the top agents in her field. She had even named her after him, "Gina". How long had their affair gone on she wondered? Was it still happening when he married Kata? After their children were born? After he started his 'fling' with her, Carla?

It was all in the file. Soon Kata would know almost everything that she knew. And she would not take him back. Carla could see in Kata's eyes that she could never do that. She was like a wounded animal. Tears swept down her face. As she stared at the photograph of Amanda and Mac together she howled. A strange alien noise with so much distress in it that it tore your very soul. But not Carla's. Long ago Mac Maconi had taken whatever soul she had and ripped it into a thousand pieces.

"Kata you have to be strong. You have to take control of this."

Kata blinked through the tears.

"How? What do I have to do?"

Carla had it all neatly planned.

"You go to Amanda. Show her the photographs. Tell her you know everything. You want the best modelling jobs. You are going to make a career for yourself again."

Kata looked unsure.

"Kata you must. You have to be self sufficient."

She nodded meekly.

"Then what."

"Go see your solicitor. File for divorce. You have all the grounds. Chances are you will be able to keep everything. His adultery outweighs anything in your prenuptial agreement. He can't stop you going back to work. You have to do that. He was going to abandon you."

Kata looked shocked, then resigned.

"I don't know who to see. We have always used Mac's man."

Carla was prepared.

"I have a name for you. Go see him. He is very good. He will fight your corner. Trust me."

Kata nodded. Carla watched the lovely figure raise her head as she hailed a taxi.

She picked up her phone.

"Giorgio?"

She smiled to herself.

"Oh yes. It all went well. Very well."

In Pursuit

❧ ❦

Elen had never driven so fast. She had hardly noticed the scenery as the car hurtled down the mountain road. Startled sheep chewed the new grass as she passed. Lambs scampered on the lower slopes. Elen was oblivious. The only thing she had on her mind was Rhys Harris. The sooner she could get to him and convince him that he was the only man in the world for her the better.

The traffic was so heavy today. Lorries heading from Swansea to Merthyr blocked the road. Why wouldn't they hurry up?

The rain was beginning to fall. The spray swirled up and muddied the wind screen. She turned right at the roundabout and headed for the main town. She pulled in a few yards from the swimming pool to check her directions. Yes, that was right. Under the bridge, right past the fire station and up to the estate on the left.

Her heart was singing.

"I love you Rhys. I do. I do. And I think you love me. Please love me, Rhys. Please do."

Tears were beginning to sting her eyes. The road wound around past farms. A few straggly goats bleated as she passed.

Up past the chemist shop. This was it. Just a little further.

Then she saw him. At the bus stop. Yes. It was definitely Rhys. Her heart skipped a beat. But who was he with? She studied the tall dark haired girl at his side. Then she watched in horror as Rhys gave her a hug and put her on the bus.

The Board Meeting

෨ ෯

"Mr Maconi" the chairman's tone was sober. This was to be expected. Mac smiled as he extended his hand. The older man did not extend his.

"Sit down."

Mac did has he was told. His mouth had gone unexpectedly dry. The water was at the far end of the table. He would wait.

"Mr Maconi, we have asked you hear today as the result of some serious allegations against you."

Mac stared in disbelief.

"Allegations? From whom? What kind of allegations?"

The older man did not raise his voice.

"It would appear that you deliberately mis lead the company about the nature of the contract with Bowen Electronics. They are under the impression that we are buying the company as a going concern."

Was that all? Mac could talk his way out of this.

"That is not all Mr Maconi. You have been exhibiting some very strange behaviour of late. Mr Leverson — would you fill everyone in please?"

Mac was unprepared for this. What was going on?

A tall sandy haired man stood up.

"I was called in by the company to investigate Mr Maconi's

activities. Staff had expressed concern. He was obviously engaging in some kind of illicit transactions. He was not himself. He was secretive, disappearing for hours without explanation. Almost wrecking the negotiations. I followed Mr Maconi for three weeks. It transpired that he was having an affair with a young girl – planning to marry her in fact – despite being already married, with children here. I have the dossier here. Affairs. Blackmail. Illegitimate children. It doesn't make pretty reading."

He passed the file to the chairman. Grim faced he scanned through it, one hand gripping the arm of the leather-bound chair. He looked up at Mac. His eyes were filled with nothing but contempt.

The colour drained from Mac's face. This wasn't right. His head was swimming.

"Is this true, Giovanni? Come now, what do you have to say for yourself?"

"No. This isn't what is supposed to be happening. You are supposed to be offering me the chance of a lifetime – a place on the board – not talking about allegations and alluding to anything being out of place."

Mac was on his feet and shouting now.

"What do you mean? A place on the board?"

Mac's composure was lost. He was ranting like a mad man.

"Don't you know that history is repeating itself? Don't you understand the part you have to play out?"

"History, Mr Maconi? What are you talking about?"

Several men were on their feet now. Mac was lunging at the chairman. Security guards appeared to restrain him.

"You can't do this. I'm Macsen. The emperor. I'm going to marry Elen Llwyddog. Don't you understand?"

"Mr Maconi. You are dismissed."

Mac was still shouting. Then he collapsed onto a chair and began to sob.

Carla walked up to him.

"Carla. Tell them. Tell them they have got it wrong."

She was calm, cold even.

"A fax came for you."

Mac raised his head. Maybe this was it. The piece in the jigsaw that would make everything turn out right.

"Read it."

"Are you sure?"

"Yes, read it, damn you. They have to know."

Carla looked down at the iceman. His hair was half across his face. His eyes were wild. He was more caveman than iceman now. She had no mercy.

"It's from your wife's solicitor. She is filing for divorce."

Desperation

❧ ❦

Elen drove around the block twice not knowing what to do. Then she decided she had to face him. She parked outside his house. There was no car in the drive. Maybe he wasn't there. She stood at the gate hesitating. Then she breathed hard, walked up the path and knocked at the door.

A round faced woman answered the door.

"Yes?"

"Is Rhys in please?"

She had the same smile as Rhys. And the same kind, sparkling eyes.

"No, sorry love. His dad has just taken him to the station."

"Station?"

"Yes. He's off to Birmingham."

Elen began to panic.

"Birmingham?"

"He's taking a job there with his uncle."

She bit her lip.

"When was that decided?"

"What? Last night. He was talking it over with his cousin. She's at university in Trefforest. He just took her to the bus stop now. Reg's brother has been offering for ages to take him on. He was dead set against it, but for some reason he just decided last night that he was giving up teaching and off he went."

"Last night?"

"Yes. I told him to borrow the car, but he said he wasn't going to be back in a while. I don't know. One minute he has his heart set on the teaching, the next….."

Elen interrupted.

"Which station Mrs Harris? Cardiff central?"

"Yes, that's right. They went a while back now."

"Thank you Mrs Harris. I've got to try to catch him."

The woman looked perplexed.

"Oh. Who shall I say called?"

"Tell him it's Elen."

Elen dived back into the car and started the engine. Soon she was round the corner and on the main road leading back towards Cardiff. The traffic lights stopped her at Mountain Ash. She tried her phone again. Still no answer.

The road twisted and turned until it came out on the roundabout connecting it with the dual carriageway. Elen didn't normally go above fifty but today she put her foot to the floor and kissed the speed limit.

Goodbyes

Mac stared in disbelief at the document on the solicitor's desk.

"You mean I could lose everything?"

The grey suited solicitor nodded glumly.

"The evidence your wife has presented is very damning. A list of affairs. An illegitimate child. Blackmail. A doctor's letter suggesting that you have lost touch with reality and have mental disorders, unreasonable behaviour…"

Mac got up and looked out of the window. The sky was a melancholy grey. "Oh, well. At least it can't get any worse."

The grey suit moved towards him.

"I'm afraid it can."

Mac spun round.

"How?"

"S-Systems are suing you for fraud."

Mac took the document in his hand and glanced through it. Then he crumpled it up and threw it to the floor.

"If you have any good news for me I will be at my grandmothers. If not don't bother to contact me."

"Mr Maconi – ignoring all of this will not make it go away…"

His words fell on deaf ears. Mac was already on his way out of the office and heading down stairs. He had to return to the one person who had been faithful to him through all of this. His beloved Bibi.

Running Away

❧ ❧

Rhys's dad parked the car and took his bag out of the boot.

"Are you sure about this son? It's all very sudden."

Rhys couldn't look at his father. How could he tell him all that had gone on, that he had lost his heart so totally to someone who was marrying someone else and that he could not bear to be anywhere where he might see her again? The pain was building up inside him. It felt as though his heart would burst.

"It's the right thing to do, Dad."

"Ok. If you are sure. You've got nearly fifteen minutes before the train goes. Do you want to go for a coffee or something?"

"No thanks Dad. I'll just wait on the platform. I don't like long goodbyes."

"Right you are then."

Rhys carried his bag to the rear entrance of the station.

"I'll see you in a couple of weeks when I've got myself settled."

"Make sure you phone your mam when you get there."

"I will."

"Rhys?"

"Yes Dad."

"You can't run away from stuff you know. You take it with you."

Rhys turned and made his way towards the platform. He could run away. He had to. He couldn't face ever seeing Elen again knowing that she belonged to someone else.

The train was already in. He found his seat and swung his bag up onto the luggage rack. Then he settled down to read his book. Another set of histories. His mother had given it to him. It covered the period from the roman invasion to their departure. He was almost at the end of it. He was reading the story of Magnus Maximus, known to the Welsh as Macsen Wledig who was declared Emperor of Rome by his troops in the 4th Century. He had just gone to Rome to defend himself against other contender and was in the process of being brought down by the Emperor Theodosius.

Rhys's phone rang again. He ended the call. That was the sixth time Elen had rung that morning. He wasn't going to talk to her. He couldn't. The pain was too raw.

A text now. He decided not to look at it.

Bibi

❧ ❧

Mac turned the handle on the old wooden door. It needed painting, he noted. As usual the door was unlocked. He didn't even know if there was a key. No one would steal from Bibi and she was afraid of no one.

The house was quiet. He walked in and made his way along the corridor to the kitchen. As he opened the door he could see his grandmother sleeping peacefully in her old armchair. He smiled. He turned around and busied himself. He would make lunch for when she woke. He put on the kettle and turned to the fridge. There didn't seem to be much in there. The milk had gone off. Was his grandmother losing her sense of smell? He looked back at her, still in her night gown. He wondered if she had been there all night. She looked cold. He walked over to her and gently stroked her hair. She was almost ice cold to the touch. Mac rubbed her hand. It was cold and stiff.

"Bibi" he said softly.

There was no reaction.

"Bibi – it's me. Its Gio."

Louder this time. Frantically he lifted her from the chair.

"Bibi. Bibi. Answer me. Bibi."

It was two hours later when a neighbour walked into the kitchen to find him rocking back and forth on the floor like a child with tears streaming down his face. The neighbour bent down and released his grip on his grandmother's lifeless body.

"She's gone Gio."

"No. No. Bibi."

"Let her go. Come on. I will call the doctor and the police."

The Station

❧　❧

Elen parked the car and jumped out without even buying a parking ticket. She had to get on to the platform. The guard wouldn't allow her through. She had to go back and get a ticket. To where? To anywhere. She didn't care. She bought a single to Treorci. The first place that came into her head. She might need that if her car got clamped.

The Birmingham train was in. It was due to leave in two minutes. Where was Rhys? Elen couldn't see him anywhere.

She tried his phone again. He hung up. Then she sent a desperate text.

"Rhys don't go. Please. I love you. Elen x"

The train's engine note changed. The guard waved his paddle. Then the train slowly inched out of the station.

Elen's view was obscured by a crowd of people who had just got off the London train and were making their way to the exit. It didn't matter. She couldn't see for tears.

She had blown it. She had let herself get side tracked by Mac and his stupid dream and now she had lost her chance with the man she knew she could be happy with.

She turned to go.

She felt a hand on her shoulder. She looked up into those wonderful cornflower blue eyes as Rhys swept her up into his arms and kissed her.

"I love you too."

"You do?"

"Yes. Are you sure this time?"

"Absolutely. I love you Rhys. I love you. I love you. And I don't care who knows it."

Given that half the station now knew it that was probably just as well.

Conclusions

❧ ❦

The chairman shook her hand.

"Congratulations Miss Theodoro."

"Thank you, Sir. I'm grateful for the opportunity."

"Not at all, you deserve this."

She beamed at the chairman.

"I understand double congratulations are in order."

Carla blushed.

"Your forthcoming wedding to Giorgio. Dark horses you two. No one had any idea you were together."

Giorgio shook his hand.

"We don't believe in mixing business with pleasure."

The chairman nodded.

"Well, I shall leave you to it. Ah, here is the boy with the name plate."

The boy was actually a young man. He polished the brass plate before fixing it to the door.

"What happened to the guy you used to work for. The one who used to be married to that top model?"

"Giovanni Maconi?"

"Yeah, that was him. They say he went barmy."

Carla watched him fix the brass screws in place.

"Yes, he lost the plot totally."

"Is it true his wife sued him for every penny he'd got?"

"Yes, I believe so."

"Why would she do that? She must be worth a fortune!"

Carla smiled.

"I guess she had her reasons. He lost everything you know, wife, girlfriend, home, family – the lot. Back living with his brother in a poky flat out in the sticks somewhere."

He gave the plate a final polish.

"Theodoro. That's a very old name. How far can you trace it back?"

Carla looked out of the window. The heat of the Milan sun was rising on misty spirals off the pavement.

"Centuries" she replied to the air. "Back to the Emperor of Rome. Theodosius."